TWO PITS AND A LITTLE MURDER

A BARKSIDE OF THE MOON COZY MYSTERY
BOOK 6

RENEE GEORGE

BARKSIDE OF THE MOON PRESS

Two Pits and A Little Murder

A Barkside of the Moon Cozy Mystery Book 6

Copyright © 2020 by Renee George

All rights reserved. No part of this publication may be reproduced, stored in a retrieval system, or transmitted, in any form or by any means, without the prior permission in writing of the copyright holder.

Any trademarks, service marks, product names or named features are assumed to be the property of their respective owners, and are used only for reference. There is no implied endorsement by the author of this work.

This is a work of fiction. All characters and storylines in this book are inspired only by the author's imagination. The characters are based solely in fiction and are in no relation inspired by anyone bearing the same name or names. Any similarities to real persons, situations, or incidents is purely coincidental.

Print Edition December 2020

ISBN: 978-1-947177-37-6

Publisher: Barkside of the Moon Press

ACKNOWLEDGMENTS

I have to thank my BFFs Michelle Freeman and Robyn Peterman for keeping me on course, and getting me to the finish line! You two are caffeine for my soul!. My sister Robbin also has to be thanked, as she beta read the crap out of this book for me and gave me great comments while on her vacation! Needless to say, I have some awesome Reggie and Nadines in my life, and I am beyond thankful.

To the fans of Lily and Smooshie, as you know, these stories are love letter"s to my obsession with whodunits and my obsession with my pit bull Kona. Thank you for taking this ride with me! <3

Last, I want to thank that hot, super charged, sexy as sin coffee for firing up the muse. Thank you, Coffee. I couldn't do this without you.

I also have to thank **Lauren Allen** of the **Missouri Pit Bull Rescue** organization for patiently answering each one of my questions about pit bull rescue (no matter how crazy they might have been). Thank you for sharing the stories of success and failure you all experience in your quest to save this wonderful breed.

I encourage everyone who loves dogs to donate to this group (www.mopitbullrescue.org) as they expand their new shelter that will allow them to house even more rescues until they can be placed in foster or forever homes.

The shelter in my books is more well-funded than real life shelters, but that is the benefit of fiction. There is not nearly enough money, volunteers, or space at most of these places to help all the pit bulls who need to be rescued. Any mistakes I may have written about "pit bull rescue" are mine and mine alone.

For my family and my friends, and my friends who have become my family.
And, of course, to my real life Smoothie, Kona the Pittie Princess. Her wiggle butt gives me life!

Sometimes, the truth can be a real killer...

When Lily Mason and her human boyfriend Parker Knowles help a friend rescue two abused pitties, they're determined to find out who abandoned the dogs in a deserted house. But the decrepit home has other secrets, too, such as the dead body in the basement.

For once, Lily hasn't stumbled upon a corpse, but Parker's buddy has—and he's arrested for murder. With the help of their friends, human and non-human alike, Lily and Parker are determined to find out what really happened. Even if it means putting their own lives in danger.

CHAPTER 1

"Put your coat on," I said, holding out Smooshie's cold-weather gear. My seventy-five-pound pit bull cocked her big head sideways, her tongue lolling out the side as if to say, "Huh?"

She was totally messing with me.

"Do you want to go outside?"

Excited, she hopped up on two feet. Her yip of joy was so high-pitched it sounded like a scream.

I shook my head and held out the vest. "As soon as you get on your coat."

She bounced back and forth, then circled my legs before shoving her nose into the neck hole. I clipped the strap under her tummy while she tucked her head between my knees and nearly knocked me off balance.

I laughed and opened the door. Smooshie bolted out into the yard, diving headfirst into the pillowy snow. She snapped her jaws, biting at the giant flakes falling down all around her.

I heard Parker approach from the hall, his warm arms slipping around me. He was five-feet eleven-inches tall, a good ten inches taller than me. Being embraced by him was like being in a warm cocoon.

Winter break at the college had begun the first week of December, just in time for our first snow. I enjoyed taking classes, but I was glad to get to spend a little extra time at the shelter these next few weeks, and extra time, of course, with Parker.

He dipped down and kissed the top of my ear. "Good morning, Lily." He looked around. "Wow. It really snowed last night."

"Ten inches, and it's still coming down," I said, sighing as he pushed my thick cinnamon–colored hair to the side and nuzzled my neck. "Be careful when you drive to the shelter."

"Jackson said he'd take his snowplow and scrape the drive," he told me.

"That's great." Jackson Drake was a contractor who had started volunteering at the shelter in July. He also happened to have a snowplow, which was super handy. I rubbed my cheek against Parker's stubbly chin as I watched Smooshie make doggy angels with abandon. "You can always take a snow day."

"Dogs and volunteers wait for one man," he countered. "Me." His blue eyes lit up with mischief. "Besides, as much as I'd like nothing more than to spend the day cozied up to the fire with you, I have to check the generators. We might need them if this weather keeps up."

We had twelve rescue pits at the new shelter and another fifteen in foster homes. "Leave Elvis with me if you want."

As if hearing his name conjured him, Parker's service dog, a blue-gray Great Dane-pit bull mix named Elvis, leaned into Parker's thigh. Parker petted his faithful boy on the head. "Go on," he said.

Elvis, who wasn't easily excitable, gave a low woof before loping out to join his sister in the snow. I smiled as Parker held me tighter.

Parker chuckled. "It's nice how Elvis is finally warming up to Smooshie."

"Two peas in a pod," I agreed.

"Just like us."

His warm breath danced along my skin, raising the tiny hairs on my neck, my skin shivering with delight. "Keep that up, and you'll definitely be late getting to the shelter this morning."

He kissed the nape of my neck. "I'm okay with being a little late."

I giggled. "Just a little, huh?"

His cellphone rang from the kitchen.

I groaned. "It's too early for good news."

Parker reluctantly let me go. "I'll be right back."

"Promises, promises." I wrapped my arms around myself. I am a werecougar, and because of my species, I tolerated the cold better than humans. But it was twenty degrees outside, and the chill was seeping into my bones. I hollered at the dogs. "You both about done?"

Smooshie started zooming back and forth while Elvis trotted to a maple tree in our front yard, hiked his leg, and let it flow. After, he headed past me into the house.

Smooshie, however, took one last opportunity to roll around in the frigid fluff.

"Okay, craze-oh," I chided. "That's why you have to wear a jacket." She barreled toward me, huffing and puffing and coughing on the freezing air. "All right. Get inside."

I closed the door behind us and took off her vest. Following her to the kitchen, I watched her go for her empty bowl.

Parker stood by the sink, the phone trapped between his shoulder and ear, while he wrote on a yellow pad we kept on the counter. His brow was furrowed. "Got it. I'll be there as soon as I can. It might be this afternoon." He paused, listening to the caller. "No problem, man. I know you'd do it for me." He ended the call and put his phone down with a heavy sigh.

"What's wrong?" I asked.

"A friend of mine needs help."

"A good friend?"

Parker rubbed his face. "Yep." He looked worried.

"Is this a bring the shovel and black trash bags kind of thing?"

He cracked a smile. "It's a rescue, Lils. Two pitties in an abandoned house."

"Sounds dangerous."

"Maybe. But I still have to go."

I walked to the counter and took my phone off the charger.

"What are you doing?"

"I'm going with you," I told him as I dialed Greer. Greer

Knowles, Parker's father, didn't mind watching Smooshie or Elvis when we couldn't take them with us. "Just let me arrange for a babysitter."

Parker didn't argue with me. Instead, he picked up his own phone, touched a contact, and put it to his ear.

"Hi, Theresa," he said. "Can you come into the shelter today? I have a rescue."

I heard her say yes before Greer picked up. "What's up?" Greer asked. There was a slight gravel to his tone that reminded me of a growling bear.

It made me smile. "Hey, Greer. How do you feel about grandpuppy duty today?"

EVEN THOUGH IT WAS ONLY TEN MILES SOUTH ON RURAL Route 3, I'd never been to or through Blaston, Missouri. I rarely went anywhere outside of Moonrise unless it was Cape Girardeau. The small town—if you could call it that—boasted a total population of fifty-four, and it had a gas station and a church. We passed a discount liquor store several hundred yards from the town sign.

"This place doesn't have a post office, but it has a liquor store," I pointed out.

Parker tightly gripped the wheel. "Technically, the liquor store is outside of the town's limits." His face was pinched with stress as he turned left on a gravel road past the Church of the Cross. Parker's tires slid on an ice patch before grabbing the rocky surface.

"I should've put on the chains," he said absently as he dropped the truck into a lower gear.

"At least we put the topper on the bed last week. I'd hate to think about the freezing wind whipping through the kennels when we take the dogs back to Moonrise."

Parker nodded. Teresa Simmons, Parker's long-time employee and our friend, had donated a lot of the inheritance from her husband's death to the pit bull rescue. The topper and the truck kennels had been one of the first purchases. This was the first time we'd gotten a chance to use them.

"The rescue is at capacity. Do you have any fosters in mind?"

Parker sighed. The lines on his forehead deepened. "All our foster families are full up," he admitted.

I put my hand on his thigh. "Let's get them now and worry about the where later."

He lifted my hand from his leg and brought it to his lips. He kissed my knuckles. "I love you."

"Love you more."

He chuckled that low and sexy tone that made my heart skip a few beats. "That's not even possible."

"Hah," I told him. "Don't be too sure about that."

We drove past a couple of houses and a few trailers, vehicles, and driveways covered in snow until he pointed at a blue truck parked outside a rundown house. Parker's buddy Darren Larson waited in his own truck in front of the shabby ranch-style home. Its white paint flaked enough to reveal the gray undertone of steel siding, a green shutter dangled from a single hinge on what I assumed was the living room window. Winter-deadened vines twisted around the front door. The thick snow made footprints leading back and forth from the front door to Darren's vehicle obvious. He got out as we pulled in and parked.

On the fifteen-minute drive to Blaston, Parker told me that both he and Darren had been part of the program that matched trained rescue dogs with veterans suffering from PTSD. That's how Parker ended up with Elvis, and it was also the inspiration for starting the pit bull rescue in Moonrise. Apparently, Parker had motivated Darren to start his own animal rescue. I was both nervous and excited to meet someone new from Parker's past.

Darren, a large man, husky in build, wore a ball cap down over his forehead, and he had on thermal coveralls. He stroked his full beard, straggly and ungroomed, as he walked to us. He extended his hand to Parker, and the two men shook before leaning in for a quick shoulder-to-shoulder tap, or what I liked to call a bro-hug.

"Damn, man. How long has it been?" Darren asked.

Parker shook his head. "Too long." Parker put his arm around me. "Darren, this is my girlfriend and partner, Lily Mason. Lily, this is Darren Larson. This guy got me through the training program."

"We helped each other," Darren said. "It's damn nice to meet you, Lily."

"Nice to meet you, too. Parker tells me you live down south in Centerville. Parker said your brother-in-law alerted you to the dogs. Does he live in Blaston?

Darren nodded. "Yeah, the house is going up for auction this week, and Rowdy and his girlfriend were looking to put a bid on the place but wanted to check it out first. See if it had bones. That's when they found the pit bulls. I know you have more experience with the breed. That's why I called you, Parker."

My gut ached. "What kind of shape are they in?"

Darren's lips thinned. "I can't rightly say. They won't let me get close." He pulled a small flashlight from his pocket. "It's dark in the basement, but I could see they were tied together at the base of the stairs."

Parker clenched his hands. "I'd like to tie up whoever did it and leave them in a dark basement."

"You and me both, brother," Darren agreed. "How do we want to approach this?"

"Carefully," Parker said. He retrieved a bowl of food, two muzzles, bolt cutters, a small bag that held protective gear, and two control poles. He handed me the items then he nodded to Darren. "Let's get the carriers and put them close to the front door."

"One of the dogs is more aggressive than the other. Seems to be the protector," Darren said.

"Then that's who we start with," I said. I headed toward the front door with the gear.

"Hey, don't go—" Darren started.

When I glanced back, I saw Parker had put his hand on his friend's shoulder. "Lily knows how to be careful."

The door was unlocked, and as I entered, I immediately noted the scents of dust and mold. I followed the sound of alert barking coming from a narrow corridor that led to an open basement door. I set down all my stuff and flipped a switch on the wall outside the basement door, but no lights came on. I heard steps behind me.

"The power doesn't work," Darren said. "The house was foreclosed back in March. Rowdy and his girl were thinking about flipping the house."

I grimaced. "In this town? How is that profitable?"

Darren shrugged. "I don't know. I love my wife, but her brother is a bit of a dumb ass."

I smiled. "Well, at least he was smart enough to call you and not try to take matters into his own hands." Speaking of hands, I unzipped the gear bag and took out a pair of bite gloves.

Darren's eyes darted back toward the front door. "Maybe Parker should go down first and assess the situation."

I could understand why Darren would think Parker should take the lead since Darren didn't know me, but he was wrong. I'd discovered during my three years at the pit bull rescue that there was something in my chemistry as a werecougar that had a calming effect on dogs. Parker said the calming extended to humans, but I didn't think it worked on any humans particularly well. Except him. But he was my mate. His mind, his soul, his body, and his scent were tied to me, not just on an emotional level but also on a cellular level.

"I'll wait for Parker if it makes you more comfortable," I offered. After all, it didn't cost me anything but a few seconds. I wasn't prideful. I grew up in a place where most folks saw me as somehow less than. I'd learned that there was no amount of getting mad about it that would get them to change their minds.

The tension at the corners of Darren's eyes eased. "Thanks. I don't mean no disrespect. The aggressive dog down there is pretty big, and you're just a slip. Hell, he might outweigh you."

I nodded as I adjusted the straps on my gloves and clipped the two muzzles to a carabiner on my coat. It was canvas on the outside and would help protect me against bites to the arms if the dogs became violent.

"What's the situation?" Parker asked as he rounded the corner.

"Just waiting on you," I replied.

"Why?" His genuine confusion was almost comical.

"I thought it would be better if you went first," Darren chimed in.

Parker chuckled. "Then you haven't seen Lily work. She's the best dog handler I've ever seen."

Darren gave me an assessing once over. He looked unconvinced.

Parker squeezed my shoulder then glanced at Darren. "Let her work."

I turned my attention to the dogs as I took a few tentative steps down the stairs. The loud barks and growls were deafening. I could smell feces, urine, along with the sour smell of infection. One of the dogs had an injury.

"Give Ryan a heads-up," I said loud enough for Parker to hear me but not so loud as to scare the dogs more.

"Already did," Parker said, his voice even and calm. "I called him before we left the house."

"Doesn't she need a flashlight?" Darren asked. He had said it quietly, and if I had been human, it would have been out of earshot.

"She's fine," Parker told him.

I smiled as I took seven more steps down, putting me three steps from the dogs. I didn't want to blind the dogs with a flashlight. They were terrified enough. Their eyes would be adjusted to the dark, and with my supernatural vision, I'd see them just fine without the extra illumination.

"Hello," I said calmly. The larger one was a solid color and had a head that rivaled Elvis's in size, and the smaller one was white with gray patches, and it was shaking with fear. "I'm not going to hurt you. You're safe now."

Under the scent of dog waste and infection, there was a slight odor of matchsticks, stale beer, and cigarette smoke, along with a few other scents I couldn't identify. Maybe the abandoned house had been used as a party place. Cautiously, I set the food down on the step just above the dogs. The larger protector growled but didn't snap or lunge. So far, so good.

I inched closer. The bigger dog began to whimper, scooting back while the little one tucked in from behind. There was a chain tethered around the lowest step and wrapped around their necks. Hot rage flared. The dog stopped whimpering and started growling again. Crap. I needed to stay relaxed if I had any hope of gaining their trust. I reined in my anger and gently tugged on the wild part of me, easing it to the surface.

"It's all right," I whispered. "You're safe. I promise."

"You doing okay?" Darren asked.

"Fine," I told him. The way the little one looked away when her gaze met mine reminded me of Elinor Dashwood in the final scene of Sense and Sensibility, the way she'd turned away from Edward Ferras when he told her his brother was the one who'd gotten married.

The larger dog gave me a warning growl. I guess he didn't like me staring at his girl. A hint of a smile played on my lips. "Don't you worry, Edward. I wouldn't harm your Elinor for any reason, and I'm going to make sure neither of you are harmed ever again."

I took his soft sigh as a good sign. I nudged the food bowl closer. Edward eyed it warily for a moment before deciding his hunger outweighed his suspicion. While his head was in the bowl, I gave him a light stroke above the ear, and when he didn't stop eating, I gave him another. "Good boy," I said softly. He was obviously used to people. Whoever had tied them to this stair was a piece of crap, but maybe before they'd wound up here, someone had shown them kindness.

I unclipped one of the muzzles as I waited for Edward to finish off the last of the morsels. He leaned into my hand, and I gave him a harder scritch at the ear, my heart exploding in my chest with a surge of protectiveness for the big fella. "I'm going to put this muzzle on you," I told him, "but it won't have to stay on long."

I knew he couldn't understand what I was saying, but the softening around his eyes let me know he wasn't going to fight me. I slipped it on with ease and looped it around the back of his head. He rested his chin on the step and waited.

Goddess, so much trust! I wanted to hug him, but I had to take care of Elinor. I added some more food in the bowl and moved it to where she could reach.

She took right to it, gobbling it down until there was nothing left but licking the bowl. Her hunger made me want to hunt someone down and chain them up for a few days without food.

"Okay, sweet girl," I told her, unclipping the other muzzle. "It's your turn."

Her tongue lolled to the side, reminding me of Smooshie. She jerked her head back when I put the muzzle to her nose, but the chain around her neck kept her from getting far. She yelped as she met the end of her tether. Edward started to whine again.

"Should we come down?" Parker asked.

"Not yet," I said. I cupped Elinor's big head, and I allowed my cougar to come forward even more, my hands and arms sprouting fur. "You can trust me, girl. I promise." I cupped her big head between my palms. Her whole body trembled, but she wasn't trying to get away anymore. She didn't try to stop me this time as I slid the muzzle onto her face. "Such a good, good girl." I gave her a gentle pat.

She licked me through the muzzle, and once again, I felt the fierce urge to protect. "Let's get you lovebirds out of here." I withdrew my cougar until I was completely human-looking again and hollered up the steps. "You can bring down the bolt cutters now. They're both muzzled."

"Damn," I heard Darren say to Parker. "She's good."

Parker chuckled. "The best."

It took a few minutes to get the chains cut. Parker and Darren had carried the dogs up the stairs and to the truck. Neither of the pits tried to fight it. I think both dogs were too exhausted to struggle. I could tell by their wary looks, though, that Edward wasn't happy about being separated into his own kennel. Neither was Elinor. But it would make the drive safer for both of them.

"Thanks for your help, Parker," said Darren. "You, too, Lily."

"I'm glad you called," said Parker. "A little TLC and these two will be right as rain."

The little one huddled into the corner, favoring her left leg. "We better get them to Ryan," I said. "I'm worried about Elinor." I half-smiled at the red-nosed boy who was staring at his friend. "I think Edward is worried about her as well."

"They do seem bonded." Parker squeezed my shoulder. "Elinor and Edward, huh?"

"I'm shooting for a happy ending," I told him.

"We'll make sure of it."

Darren chuckled. "You two be sure and invite me to the wedding."

My eyes widened. Parker shook his head. "We are happily cohabitating."

I nodded emphatically. "Super happy."

Parker and I had discussed the idea of marriage a few times. We were mates. My witch-shifter ancestry made that a certainty. That was stronger than any legal contract.

"All right." Darren put his hand up in front of him. "I get it. I'm just glad to see Parker's found someone. If your half as good with people as you are with dogs, then my friend is a lucky man."

My cheeks warmed. "Thanks. Welp, we better get on the road. It was nice meeting you."

"Right back at you, Lily," Darren said.

"You all should come by for dinner. Mia would love to meet you and Lily."

Parker's brow furrowed. "Tonight?"

"No," Darren said. "Mia has the night shift at the hotel where she works tonight. Besides, I'll be doing a little recon."

"What do you mean?"

"Nothing dangerous," he assured Parker. "Just going to set up some motion cameras to see if I can catch whoever put those poor pitties in the basement."

"Don't go confronting them on your own," Parker said.

"I won't." He raised three fingers. "Scout's honor."

Parker laughed. "That would be great if you were ever a Scout."

"I promise I won't put myself in harm's way." Darren shrugged. But I hope I can catch them assholes doing something that I can give to the police."

Parker nodded. "Okay."

"Call us," I said. "For dinner, I mean. We'll set up a night."

He smiled. "Sounds like a plan."

Parker and I got in the truck. He glanced at me. "Let's go get our lovers their happily ever after."

I scootched across the seat and rested my head on his shoulder. He kissed my forehead.

Since my friend Nadine had gotten pregnant, she'd made

me watch every Jane Austin movie, and with Christmas right around the corner, she'd also introduced me to Lifetime Movie romance binges. I'd tolerated them at first for her sake, but I had to admit, I'd grown pretty fond of easy resolutions.

I sighed contentedly. "I do love a happy ending."

CHAPTER 2

Nadine Booth, one of my best friends, rubbed her rounded belly. "I can't believe how big I'm getting. It hasn't even been five months." She groaned as she flopped down on her couch and put her feet up on an ottoman.

Other than the stomach pooch, I thought she was looking thin. "You're lucky it's a human pregnancy," I said. "If you were a shifter, you would be much further along."

Her eyes widened. "Are you kidding me? I already feel full term." Earlier this year, Nadine had learned that me and my Uncle Buzz were cougar shifters. For the most part, she'd taken the news that there was an entire paranormal world unknown to humans rather well.

"You have three babies in there. They are bound to need a little kicking room."

Uncle Buzz walked in from the kitchen, holding a mug of herbal tea. His red hair was sticking up in the back, his beard unkempt, and his eyes carried weariness. "Here you go, darling," he said to Nadine. "Do you need anything else?"

She took the tea that Buzz offered her.

"Are you feeling any better?" he asked her, evident concern in his gaze.

"I'm still pukey," she told him. "But thinking about something else helps." The pregnancy, so far, had been rough on Nadine. Morning sickness had caused her to drop some weight, and our friend Reggie, who was monitoring her progress, had said that she needed to eat a lot more calories.

Buzz didn't look much better.

I narrowed my gaze at him. "What's going on, Buzz? You look like Hell. Are you experiencing Couvade Syndrome?"

His expression turned bland. Nadine looked at me. "Couvade what?"

"Sympathetic pregnancy," I explained. "Where the father shares pregnancy symptoms with the mother."

He raised a brow, clearly annoyed with me for pointing out that something was going on with him. "I've been working extra shifts at the diner to cover for Freda. She's cut back on her hours to watch Lacy's boy."

Buzz gave me a barely imperceptible head shake. He was lying to Nadine about why he was rundown. Working a few extra shifts would not affect a shifter in the same way as a human. Buzz's exhaustion was from something else. Something he didn't want Nadine to know about. I let out a small sigh. I would let it go for now, but I fully intended to corner my uncle the next time I got him alone. He and Nadine were partners. She was having his babies. She deserved his honesty.

"How are those pups you rescued from Blaston yesterday?" Buzz asked, definitely changing the subject.

"Blaston?" Nadine put her feet on the floor and leaned forward. "Now there's a hole in the wall."

I nodded. "Not much there, that's for sure." I glanced at Buzz then back to Nadine. "We got a call from Parker's friend, Darren Larson. He owns a rescue in the next county over. His brother-in-law, a guy named Rowdy, was looking to buy an abandoned house there in Blaston and found two pit bulls tied to the bottom step of the basement stairs."

Buzz scrubbed his beard. "People suck."

"Hey," Nadine said. "I'm people."

A sly smile perked up the corners of Buzz's lips.

Nadine barked a laugh and threw a decorative pillow at him. She turned her attention to me. "Are the dogs okay?" Her eyes were suddenly glistening with tears. "It really is awful."

"They will both be fine," I told her, hoping it was the truth. "Elinor has a femur fracture and some sores on her sides. Edward is malnourished, but otherwise, healthy."

Nadine sniffled then smiled. "I knew you liked Sense and Sensibility."

I laughed. "You're rubbing off on me."

Her expression grew distant for a moment. "Did you say Rowdy?"

"Yes." I nodded. "Interesting name."

Nadine snorted. "If it's the Rowdy I think it is, the name fits him like a pair of Spanx."

"Uncomfortably?" I asked.

She laughed. "No. The Rowdy I knew was a shit-stirrer and a lech. At least, he used to be. I dated a guy named Alex

Naples, who was friends with Rowdy, and Rowdy made more than one pass at me."

"How long ago was this?" Buzz asked with interest.

Nadine waved a hand at him. "High school," she said. "Nothing for you to worry about."

He dipped down and kissed her soundly. "Darlin', I am not worried."

"Awfully confident," she teased.

He gave her hip an affectionate pat. "That I am." He kissed her again. "I better get going. Leon won't be able to handle the lunch rush on his own."

Leon Driscoll, Buzz's part-time help since Freda cut back her hours, was a young, black man from Springfield who had moved to Moonrise for college. He was studying to get a two-year degree in nuclear medicine technology. The program received hundreds of applicants but only took twelve students every cycle. Leon had won the spot over some pretty stiff competition.

Nadine gave Buzz a worried smile. "Don't work too hard."

"You know me." He grabbed his coat from a hook near the front door.

I muttered low enough so that only Buzz could hear me. "We *will* talk later."

He frowned as he opened the front door, stopped, stooped down, and turned back into the house with a package in his hand. "Looks like you got something in the mail."

Nadine jumped up from the couch. "Hey, don't touch my box!"

Buzz chuckled. "That's not what you said last night."

She blushed, her grin wide, as she crossed the room and took the parcel from him. "Christmas is right around the corner." She leaned into his arms and poked his chest playfully. "Any boxes that aren't an actual part of me are off-limits to you, mister."

"Fair enough." He gave her forehead a peck. "Best get going."

Nadine nodded, and I could feel her reluctance as the man she loved with her entire being walked out the door.

She watched from the window as he trudged to his car and pulled out onto the street before she turned to me. "You're worried about him, aren't you?"

"He looks tired," I said, trying to minimize her anxiety. "I'm sure it's all the work."

"Will you talk to him?" She set the parcel down on her coffee table. "He won't talk to me about it. I know he's trying to protect me, but I'm a tough cookie. He could tell me if he was sick. Does your kind get sick like that? I mean, I know when Buzz wasn't turning into a cougar, it had really taken its toll."

Buzz went cold turkey on shifting into his cougar form for four months before spending another whole month in California with a shifter fertility specialist harvesting his swimmers so he could have a child with Nadine. Shifters only mated with shifters, at least that's the way it had always been before science had intervened. Buzz's dedication to not shift even when the urge was unbearable had caused severe mood swings verging on rage.

For a man who'd exercised extreme control for the past fifty or so years of living among humans, he'd been the most surprised when he'd punched one of the biggest jerks in town. In front of a diner full of witnesses. When the jerk was murdered, Buzz's assault had made him the prime suspect. That, and Buzz had been seen fleeing the scene. Not a great combination when trying to stay low-key and off human radar.

However, he'd done it for love. Even without the mating scent, even with Nadine being human, Buzz had grown to love her with a feeling so deep he'd been willing to risk exposure to make her happy. Basically, the opposite of how he'd told me to act when I first arrived in Moonrise. The memory made me smile.

"I'll talk to him," I reassured Nadine.

"And you'll tell me if there's something serious going on," she added.

I grimaced. Would I tell her? I hated to keep anything from Nadine, especially now that she knew our secrets. It had taken her a few weeks to come to grips with the fact that Buzz and I were something other than human. She'd been angry with Buzz, questioning everything about their relationship. It had been different for Parker and me. I'd come out before we'd started dating.

Literally.

I changed into a cougar in front of him to save us both from being killed by a murderer.

He'd kept his distance from me for several months.

However, he'd also kept my secret. But the point of the matter was, his eyes were wide open when we got together. Nadine dated Buzz for a year, moved in with him, and started planning for a family before she'd found out about his supernatural status. It was enough to rock even a reasonably strong foundation, and it had taken her a while to trust him again.

Still, I had a witch ancestor whose ability was truth-saying. A power that made it impossible for anyone around her to say anything other than the unvarnished truth. My ancestor's ability had made her less than popular, and she'd been killed because a lot of folks are ugly on the inside, and they don't like it when they are forced to speak their innermost thoughts out loud.

A few years back, I discovered that some of her magic had been passed down to me. I couldn't compel someone to tell the truth. Not like my ancestor had. But people who were tired of keeping secrets found themselves sharing these secrets whenever they were around me. And the ones who wanted to keep their secrets hidden, well, I always knew when they were lying. Knowing I possess this magic made me careful about protecting the privacy of those around me, especially the people I loved.

"If there is something serious going on, I'll make sure Buzz tells you."

Nadine plopped down on the couch. "I can live with that."

My phone dinged. I pulled it out of my purse and looked at the text. "Ryan wants to see me."

"About work?"

I shook my head. "The two rescues from yesterday."

"Go," Nadine said. "I'll be fine."

"Do you want to come with me?"

"Nah," she told me. "This is my only day off this week, and I'm going to put my feet up and catch up on some of my shows."

"Sounds like a good plan." I strolled to Nadine and gave her a firm hug. "Call me if you need anything."

She patted my shoulder. "You worry too much."

I smiled as we parted. "That's probably true."

Petry's Pet Clinic was located on the northeast side of town. The renovations to the new building and parking lot were finished, and the place looked as fancy as Ryan's sports car. I pulled my truck around the side to the employee lot and parked. I was anxious to see how Elinor and Edward were doing. Parker had been making calls all morning trying to find someone to foster the pair of them, but he'd struck out.

Abby Levine, Ryan's receptionist, grinned when I walked in. Abby was a petite black woman with her hair short and slicked close to her head. Her pale blue scrubs were neatly pressed and immaculate. Even with her rigorous attention to detail when it came to her appearance, Abby gave off a real warmth that put customers at ease. "Hey Lily," she said, her voice breathy. "I thought you were off today."

"Ryan texted," I told her. I worked at the clinic part-time for experience and college credits as I worked toward my degree. Ryan let me set my schedule, which helped tremendously when my caseload at the college got heavy.

"Oh, must be about those two sweeties in the back. Poor things are clinging to each other." She shook her head. "Some folks need a good kick in the backside."

I nodded. "I know just the foot for the job."

She laughed. "Me too."

I walked through reception to the clinic and headed to the isolation room. Ryan checked out all our rescue pit bulls on intake, and he was extremely intuitive when it came to knowing what they needed. And the state Elinor and Edward had been in, he would know they needed a quiet place away from the chaos.

The VTA, veterinarian technology assistant, Kelly, a woman with bright red hair and wearing pink scrubs, carried a giant Maine Coon cat named Tiger to the scales.

She exhaled heavily as she put him down. "My gosh, this boy is huge." She blinked as the digital monitor beeped. "Twenty-three pounds."

Tiger had been coming in every few months to have his diabetes monitored.

"Did he gain a pound?"

Kelly nodded, her expression pained. "I do not want to give Lev another lecture about what he's feeding her." She gave me an appraising look. "You wouldn't want to handle it, would you?"

I laughed. "Not on your life." Lev Nelson was a nice old man but explaining anything to him was like talking to a three-year-old. Lots of "why" questions, without a whole lot of caring about the answers. "I'm off duty today."

She harrumphed as she picked up Tiger and cradled the fur baby. "He is the cuddliest cat."

"That's because he's too fat to do anything else," said Ryan as he came out of the back. "Hey, Lily." He put his hand on my shoulder and directed me to the isolation room.

His light brown hair, as usual, was perfectly coiffed, framing his movie-star looks. All the women in town swooned around Ryan Petry. Unfortunately for them, he was gay. His sexual preference wasn't public knowledge, but he was out to his close friends, and recently, he'd gotten the nerve up to tell his mom and dad. He told me that his mother hugged him, and his father asked if he was still on for Sunday golf. All in all, a good result.

"Is something wrong?" I asked as we went inside the space. Elinor and Edward welcomed me with tail wags. I pressed my fingers to my chest. "Are Elinor and Edward in worse shape than you thought initially?"

Ryan's lips pursed in consternation. "They'll be fine. Elinor's break was an easy set, but I'm concerned about the infection on her side. She has some missing hair and sores."

"Sarcoptic Mange?" I gave him a sharp look. Sarcoptic Mange was caused by scabies-like parasites that burrowed under dogs' skin, causing intense itching. It could be transmitted to humans and other animals. I'd have to pick up some scabies medication for Parker and me, and we'd have to call Darren as well. We did not want scabies running rampant through the volunteers or the rescues.

"No." Ryan scratched his arm reflexively. "I've done a few skin scrapings from several of the affected areas, and I couldn't find any parasites under the microscope."

"Then what do you think it is?"

He peered at me. "Did you notice anything in the basement that would have indicated drugs were made there?"

"Do you think this is drug-related?" I thought back to the basement. "Some beer bottles and stale cigarette smell." I tried to think of all the different odors. My brother smoked a lot of pot, but I hadn't detected any hint of marijuana. "Oh, and there was a strong scent of matchsticks."

He frowned. "Red phosphorous."

"I don't think I've ever smelled red phosphorous."

"It's similar to matchsticks since the striking part is made with phosphorous."

"Is that important?"

"Maybe. Red phosphorous is used in the cooking process of methamphetamines." His frown deepened. "If the dogs were exposed to meth, they could be facing some real challenges."

"Like what?"

"Central nervous system damage, lung damage, and withdrawal. Elinor's sores might have resulted from fume exposure."

"Is there any way to know for sure?"

"Did you see any equipment?"

"It was dark, but the basement looked empty. If anyone had been making drugs down there, they moved their set-up before they abandoned the dogs." I clenched my fists. "It's reprehensible."

"Maybe there was still some stuff down there they wanted to protect," Ryan said. "They might've planned to get the dogs later."

"If that's true, they'll get caught. Parker's friend Darren posted cameras around the place to try and catch whoever tied the pit bulls in the basement. If they go back to that abandoned house, he'll get them on video."

Ryan knelt in front of the kennel. He pulled treats from his pocket and fed one to each of the dogs. Elinor still trembled, and I wondered if it was fear or a side effect of her exposure.

"What can we do to help them?" I asked.

"I want to keep them another night. They're eating well, and that's a good sign." He smiled as Edward licked his fingers. "They really are friendly."

"How would you feel about fostering them?" I asked.

Ryan's mouth dropped open. He chuckled. "My two cats would never forgive me."

"Oh, I don't know." I grinned at him. "Pitties love kitties." At least, Smooshie and Elvis loved me.

"Unfortunately, my cats hate everyone." He shook his head. "Including me at times."

I giggled. "All right. But I'm sure that's not true."

"I better get back to it. I have a neutering to do."

I stared at Elinor and Edward. "They have to be okay."

Ryan nudged my shoulder. "I'll take good care of them, Lily. And if you are having trouble finding them a place right away, I'm happy to keep them here for a few more days."

I let out a relieved breath. I felt better knowing he'd keep an eye on them while they recovered. "Thanks, Ryan."

I couldn't stop thinking about the basement. I hadn't searched it when we'd rescued the dogs. Maybe I had missed something important. I'd ask Parker to call Darren and ask if anyone showed up on his cameras yet.

"You know, it wouldn't take me long to run out to the house we found them in and take a peek around. Just to confirm the meth theory. I mean, it could help Elinor if you knew for sure, right?"

"Yes," he said, narrowing his gaze. "But don't go looking for trouble, Lily."

I smiled. "Since when have you known me to go looking for trouble?"

"Never mind. You don't have to look for it. Trouble finds you."

The truth in that statement made me squirm. "I'll do a quick in and out in the broad light of day."

His face pinched with worry. "Maybe you should take Parker with you."

Ryan was one of the few people in our tight circle who didn't know about mine and Buzz's supernatural status, but I believed that even if he had known I could shift into a vicious cougar, he would have still worried about me. It's one of the many reasons I adored him.

"I'll call Parker and see if he's available to go with me." Parker didn't have the volunteer staff to cover at the shelter today, so I knew he wouldn't be able to make it, but I'd still call him.

Ryan seemed to read my mind. "If he can't make it, take Nadine."

"I don't want to expose her to any drug-related residue or fumes."

He pursed his lips. "She can always wait out in the truck." He gave me a flat stare. "You know, with her gun."

I choked back a laugh. I was as lethal as any gun, but still, I nodded. "If Parker can't go, I'll ask Nadine."

"Promise," he said.

"Cross my heart," I told him.

"Then, yes," he finally said. "It would help to know for sure if Elinor's wounds are because she was exposed to drug fumes."

I gave him a peck on the cheek. "I'm on it."

CHAPTER 3

"Thanks for leaving your house for me," I told Nadine when she climbed in the truck. Parker, as I'd suspected, couldn't get away from the shelter today. He said he would call Darren and see if anyone went into the house since yesterday and get back to me. I kept my promise to Ryan and called Nadine, and she had been gracious enough to give up her full day of binge-watching her shows to join me.

Nadine wore a puffy forest green parka that made her look even more pregnant and a winter cap with faux-furry earmuffs. Add to that her fuzzy knee-length boots, and she was ready for a blizzard.

She patted down her coat, and I could see her holster peaking from the left pocket.

"I sure hope Ryan is wrong about the drug lab," Nadine said when she got herself settled in. "We've busted up five of them in our county this year, but we don't have the same kind of meth numbers as some of the surrounding counties. Even so, it's probably a good idea to check it out."

"I appreciate the back-up, but I don't want you going inside. If there's any fumes or whatever, and you get sick from it, Buzz will never forgive me."

"I'm a deputy sheriff, Lils. It's my job."

"Not today, it isn't. Today, you are my very pregnant friend, who just happens to be carrying a really big gun."

She giggled. "It's not that big. I brought my back-up piece, a subcompact 9mm. I usually have it strapped to my ankle."

"Might want to invest in a holster that hits you a little higher up," I teased. "Pretty soon, you won't be able to bend down to get your gun."

"You are the worst friend," she said with mock hurt.

"Ha!" I shook my head. "And you're the best."

She grinned. "It's warmer than I thought it would be."

"It's twenty-eight degrees outside. Below freezing."

"Your truck heater must be really good."

It wasn't. "I think your hormones are messing with your internal temperature gauge."

She gave me a worried smile. "I'd roast alive if it meant having these babies."

"They will be beautiful," I told her as we drove out of town, south toward Blaston. "With you and Buzz as the parents, they'll be downright gorgeous."

"Reggie says my pregnancy is progressing as expected. I know she's worried about me not eating, but I swear I'm trying. I feel fine except when I eat. When I eat, I feel sick. I've been drinking protein shakes. I can keep them down most of the time." She made a face. "Sometimes Buzz comes home smelling of burgers and grilled onions. I swear, it's like getting hit in the face with a nausea bomb."

"You should ask him to shower when he gets home."

"He does, but, and this is going to sound awful, I can still sometimes smell it in his beard."

"I've never noticed." And I had a keen nose. "Doesn't he shampoo his beard?"

"Yes," she said, "But my sense of smell has become super intense since last month. I think it might be the reason I get sick so easily."

"I've always had a heightened sense of smell because of the whole werecougar aspect." I gave her a sly side glance. "Maybe your pregnancy is turning you into a shifter."

She jerked her gaze to me. "That's impossible, right?"

I smirked. "Yes. It's impossible. Humans can't be turned into shifters."

I'd been teasing her, but the look of disappointment on her face made me a little sad. She knew we lived a long time. Much longer than humans. I worried about that sometimes for Parker and myself, but I hadn't really thought about how Nadine must feel.

"You are the love of Buzz's heart," I told her. "And he is going to love you as long as you'll have him, and even longer than that. But he is in his eighties—even though he doesn't look like it, which means, he's going to start aging bit by bit, and you are in your twenties, so really, the two of you couldn't be more perfectly matched."

Some of the tension eased from her shoulders. "Buzz told me something to that effect." She stared out the window as we passed pastures of pure white then laughed. "I still find it hard to believe at times that Buzz is technically a senior citizen." She pointed ahead. "We're coming up on Blaston."

I saw the liquor store about a half-mile ahead. "Gotta love landmarks." There were two beat-up trucks, one a half-ton and one a mini, and a red, four-door Pontiac in the parking lot. "Quite the crowd for a Monday afternoon," I said.

Nadine shook her head and smiled. "It's five o'clock somewhere." She gazed up ahead, her eyes unfocused as if in thought, then said, "I haven't been out here in a few years. Last time was a domestic disturbance call. The wife had stabbed her abusive husband." She sighed. "He lived. She got probation."

"Did they stay together?" I put on my blinker after we entered the town and turned down a gravel road to the abandoned house.

"Once the trial was finished, she took off. I think he moved back here. But honestly, I don't know what happened to him after he got out of the hospital. I've never had to take another call about him."

I gripped the steering wheel. Theresa Simmons, Parker's office manager, had been married to such a man, and I hoped if there was an afterlife for humans, that he was burning in Hell for all he'd put her through. I had a lot of hate in my soul for men who abused women. These were the same jerks who abused children and animals. Sometimes I wished I could mete out shifter justice on them. Mostly because human justice did so little to punish abusers who did things like chain two dogs in an abandoned house and leave them to starve to death.

I pulled into the parking lot of the aforementioned abandoned home. There was a blue truck in the driveway.

"Someone's here," Nadine said.

"That's Darren's truck," I told her. "Maybe he drove over after Parker called him. I plucked my phone out of the cup holder and tapped on Parker's name in my call log. He picked up on the first ring.

"You make it there?" he asked.

"Just here," I replied. "Did Darren tell you he was going to meet me at the house? His truck is parked out front."

"No," Parker said. "I left a message telling him what you planned, but he never called me back. Maybe he skipped the middleman and decided to meet you there."

I turned off the engine. "Maybe."

"Let me know what you find out," he said. "And be careful."

"All right. I'll call you in a bit." I hung up.

Nadine gave me a look. "I'm going in with you."

I placed my hand on her arm. "Stay put. Darren's in there. I'll be fine. If anyone suspicious shows up, honk the horn."

Nadine shook her head and smirked. "I've always wanted to be the lookout."

"Really?"

"Nope. Not even a little."

I gave her a soft punch in her puffy covered arm. "I'll be back in a minute."

"If you run into trouble, holler," she said.

"If I run into trouble, I won't be the one hollering."

Nadine choked on a laugh. "Just don't eat anyone's face off."

I grinned. "I would never." I put my phone in my coat pocket. The doggie poop bags I kept in my pocket for Smooshie crinkled against it. I got out of the truck then headed up to the front door. It was cracked open, but still, I knocked.

"Darren," I called out. "Are you in here?"

He didn't answer, so I went inside and called again. "Darren? It's Lily. Lily Mason. Parker's friend." I was loud enough in the empty house that the sound of my voice was hollow as it bounced around the narrow hallway as I walked toward the basement door.

I heard the thud of heavy footfalls coming from the basement. My stomach knotted. It could be Darren. Or it could be whoever imprisoned Elinor and Edward. Maybe they'd knocked Darren on the head, and that's why he didn't answer when I'd yelled his name. I skirted the door and waited to one side, ready to pounce on any threat.

The steps creaked as someone made their way up the stairs. When they closed in on the door, I could faintly hear music playing. Heavy Metal.

The door swung open. My claws bit into my palms as I reflexively curled my fingers into tight fists. A flannel-clad, tall and broadly built man stepped out, his back to me. I shoved him hard, and he went flying to the ground, cursing as he rolled up on a knee. His eyes met mine as he yanked earbuds from his ears.

"What the hell?" he shouted. It was Darren.

Oh boy.

And he was pissed.

"I'm so sorry," I apologized. "I called for you, and when you didn't answer, I thought..." I grimaced. "I don't know what I thought." I extended my hand to help him, but he was already using the wall to brace himself as he managed to get to his feet. "Did I hurt you?"

He rubbed his hands and wrists, no doubt sore from the landing. "I'm fine." He narrowed his gaze on me. "What are you doing here?"

I jammed my hands into my pockets and touched my phone as if it were a lifeline. "One of the dogs, Elinor, might have been exposed to drug fumes. I wanted to see if there were any signs of a lab in the basement. It would help narrow down what type of treatment she needs."

He took his beanie off and rubbed his bald head. The anger eased from his voice. "That's the small one, right? With the sores on her side."

"Yes." I raised my hands, palms up. "Parker called you and left a message. When I saw you were here, I just assumed you got the message."

Darren shook his head. "I dropped my phone on the concrete last night when I got home. I bought a cheap one at the store and had to reset all the cameras to sync up to it." He half-smiled. "Because the cameras are cheap, too. They don't have any memory to speak of, so you need to have them tied to a phone through the app in order to get any footage. The app sends an alert to my phone when motion or people are detected. I want to make sure I don't miss those jokers coming back here."

"You have cameras in the basement?"

He nodded. "I have six of them I've put in the basement and in a few concealed places in the house. Also, one in the front yard and one in the back. I'm planning on nailing the bastards."

"With a hammer?"

He gave me a sharp look then barked a laugh. "You're funny."

"I'm a laugh riot," I said dryly, then cracked a smile. "Did you see anything in the basement that looked like there was a drug operation here?"

Darren shook his head. "It's pretty empty down there."

"Is it okay if I take a look around in the basement just for my own peace of mind?"

He frowned. "Go ahead. Try not to disturb the camera. I have it set up to capture anyone who goes down there."

"Thanks." I pulled my phone out and hit the flashlight feature to light my way as I headed down the steps. The basement was sparse. The beer cans were still there. I walked around and found a few empty crates. A large kitty litter box sat on the floor, under the only window, a small, high one at the back of the basement. I knelt down for a closer look and sniffed. Kitty litter was designed to conceal strong odors, but it couldn't hide stuff from a nose like mine. But it didn't smell the way I expected. It was more of a combination of eggs and vinegar. So weird. I turned the light around the room. There was a scrap of fabric in the corner. It had red marks, and it smelled like matchsticks. Was this the phosphorous Ryan had talked about? Or something else?

I took out the dog waste bag in my pocket and used it to pick up the rag, bagged it, and tucked it away in my coat. Someone smarter than me would have to analyze it. Maybe Nadine would know how to tell if it was the chemical used for processing methamphetamines.

Honk! Honk! Honk!

Nadine! She was my lookout, and the three warning blasts from my truck's horn had me sprinting to the stairs.

As I exited the house, I heard her shout, "You best stand back unless you want a chest full of hot lead to go with that hot temper."

"What are you doing in Blaston?" A thin man with creases so deep in his cheeks they looked like healed cuts stood outside a red Pontiac. The same one I'd seen parked at the liquor store. He had three other men behind him, and two of them had shotguns. The guy who spoke had a hip holster with a pistol, but I was certain he wasn't any kind of lawman. Unless he was a cop from another county. In our county of Remir, we only had the sheriff's department. "You got no business coming in here and buying up our property," the man said.

Darren was about fifteen feet from Nadine, his hands up. "Nobody here is trying to do that, pal. We're leaving if you let us."

Nadine gave him a thanks–but–I–got–this look. She held up a badge. "I'm Deputy Sheriff Nadine Booth. My partner and I," she gestured to me, "are responding to a tip that there is a drug lab on–site."

"Don't you need a warrant for that deputy?" the man asked.

Good question. Did we?

"I don't need a warrant to search an abandoned property," she said with cool confidence. "Now, you and your pals get back into your vehicles and vacate the premises right this minute, or I will assume you are connected to our investigation."

The man seemed to mull his options for a few seconds until he finally turned around and got into his car. His three cronies followed his lead. Both Nadine and Darren sighed as the vehicles drove up the gravel road and disappeared out on the main road.

Nadine sagged against my truck.

I dashed to her. "Are you all right?"

"Fine," she said. "The adrenaline rush has made me light–headed, is all."

Darren joined us. "Lady, that was badass. And I did two tours in the Middle East. I know badass when I see it."

Nadine gave him a tight smile. "I was glad you came out when you did. It gave them pause."

"Do you know who they were?" I asked.

Nadine nodded. "Larry Johnson was the leader. He's part of the riffraff in this area. I was on a bust a few years ago where he was arrested along with a few others for piecing out and reselling stolen vehicle parts."

"He didn't recognize you," I said.

"I was in uniform then and a lot less globe–like."

I laughed. "Well, I don't think he'll forget you now."

"That's probably not a good thing."

A big, black SUV, full–sized, came up the road. The

windows were tinted, and it was hard to see the driver. My body went on full alert.

"New arrival," I hissed.

Nadine gripped her weapon tighter. "Let them come," she challenged.

"Hold up," Darren said. "It's just my brother-in-law, Rowdy."

Nadine's groan was low enough that I was sure I was the only one who heard it as a lanky man with dark brown hair, wearing a cowboy hat, jeans, pointy-toed boots, and a suede and fur-lined winter coat stepped out of the driver side.

"Mia wanted to find you," he said to Darren as he looked back at his SUV. "She's been trying to call." His gaze pivoted to me, then to Nadine. And after a few barest moments of recognition, he added, "Well, I'll be, if it's not Nadie the Hottie."

Nadine looked at me, panic in her eyes. "Can we go home now?"

CHAPTER 4

"You are still pretty as a picture," the guy said. He tipped his cowboy hat in my direction, a sly grin making his top lip thin out and almost disappear. A woman crawled out the other side of the SUV.

"Rowdy Barnes, leave them girls alone." She had curly, blonde hair, and pleasant curves. I thought she was his girlfriend, the one Darren had mentioned the day before, but then the woman snapped her fingers at Rowdy and said, "Where are your manners? Momma taught us better than that."

"No, she didn't," Nadine muttered.

Rowdy wasn't cowed by his sister, but at least he shut up.

The woman's bright blue eyes were curious as she looked us over and saw Nadine brandishing a gun. "Darren, introduce me to your friends."

He pointed to me. "This is Lily. Parker's girl. The one I was telling you about."

Her face went from curious to elated, and she walked toward me. "I can't believe I'm finally getting to entertain one of Darren's friends. He never brings anyone home." She hugged me. As a shifter, I was used to physical gestures like hugs and playful punches as a way to express myself, so the spontaneous affection hadn't bothered me.

The blonde beamed me a smile. "I'm Mia. Darren's wife. He says you and Parker are coming for dinner this weekend."

It was news to me that we'd firmed up a date, but I nodded. "I'm looking forward to it."

"And who's your armed friend?"

"Nadine Booth," I told her.

Nadine holstered and pocketed her weapon. She thrust out her hand to stave off a stranger's embrace. Nadine didn't mind hugs from family and friends, but she wasn't touchy-feely with everyone.

"What have you been up to since high school, Nadine?" Rowdy asked.

I didn't like the way he was looking at my pregnant friend, and I had to fight the urge to defend her. After all, it wasn't like Rowdy was attacking her. He was a creep, not a threat. Still, I positioned myself next to her in case she needed me.

"I'm a deputy sheriff," Nadine answered flatly. She unconsciously patted her gun pocket.

I smirked when Rowdy blanched.

"I wouldn't mess with her," Darren said. "She's scary."

"Damn straight," Nadine agreed.

"How are those dogs doing?" Mia asked, shifting the focus away from her brother. "I was glad Racine called us. Lord knows Rowdy wouldn't."

"I would, too," Rowdy said. He pulled the tip of his hat down and toed a piece of gravel with his fancy boots.

"Well, I'm just glad they were found," said Mia. She looped her arm with Darren's. "Our Bear is the sweetest boy. It breaks my heart that there are people who are so cruel."

I assumed Bear was Darren's Elvis. "I feel the same."

A blue sports car with mag wheels and a loud engine pulled up next to the SUV. The tires slid on the snow before coming to a complete stop. A slender woman with dark hair wearing a white ski jacket, red leggings, and white furry boots got out.

"Hi, y'all," she greeted as she strolled to Rowdy. She draped her hand on his shoulder and leaned into him for a kiss. "Babe, what's taking so long? You promised to take me shopping in Moonrise. And you also promised to take me to Dally's Tavern & Grill for dinner tonight." She turned her focus on Nadine and me. "I'm so behind on Christmas presents."

I shrugged. "Well, then you all should go on. Nadine and I have to get back anyhow."

Nadine's shoulders sagged. She'd been on high alert since the men with guns had left, and though she wouldn't say it, I could see she was eager to leave Blaston.

Mia cast Racine an annoyed glance then smiled at me. "Let me get your number." She pulled out her phone, unlocked the screen, and pulled up her texts. "Here, just send yourself a text from me."

"I'm off," Rowdy said. "Mia, you okay catching a ride home with Darren?"

Darren nodded. "I'm done here."

Mia's smile widened. "See you two later."

Racine got in her car, Rowdy got in his vehicle, and he followed Racine as she backed up and drove away.

Mia's phone had several saved texts from Darren, Rowdy, and someone named Elle, along with numbered texts that I recognized as credit card alerts. I hit the plus at the top, typed in my number, and sent myself a "This is Mia's phone," text message. My pocket beeped as it was received.

"Got it," I told her.

Mia happily took her phone back. "I'll message you with time and directions for Friday."

I tried to think if I was busy on Friday or not. I worked at Petry's Pet Clinic in the morning that day, and I had some inventory at the rescue in the afternoon, but as far as I knew, Parker and I were free in the evening. "It's a date," I told her.

"Any special food needs, like allergies, I should know about?" she asked.

"No allergies, and I'll eat just about anything. So will Parker."

Nadine snorted. "Make sure you fix a lot. Lily's got two hollow legs."

I side-eyed my friend. "Whatever you have will suit me

just fine, in type and amount. It was really nice to meet you, Mia, and I'm looking forward to Friday." It was only three in the afternoon, but the sky was turning a dark gray, and I still needed to get the rag that I'd found to Ryan before the clinic closed. I patted Nadine on the shoulder. "Let's get you home."

AT NINE-FORTY THAT EVENING, I WAS IN MY JAM-JAMS AND snuggled against Parker on the couch as the fireplace crackled with life. Smooshie and Elvis were sharing the giant memory foam dog bed I'd bought for Elvis. I'd gotten Smooshie a smaller one, but she nearly always chose to sleep next to her big brother. They were family now, and it made me happy.

"What would we have done if Elvis and Smooshie hadn't gotten along?" I asked.

"Elvis gets along with everyone," Parker said. His tone was warm and buttery as he lazily stroked my hair.

"Tough day?" I asked.

"Just thinking about Edward and Elinor."

"We'll find a place for them," I said.

"I hope so. They're bonded, and I hate the idea of separating them, but I couldn't find anyone who'd take them both. I have one foster who can take one but not the other." His chest deflated as he sighed. "I'm glad Ryan is willing to keep them a few extra days, but they can't stay at his clinic indefinitely. I'm afraid we might have to split them up."

"We'll make sure that doesn't happen. We'll find a way to keep them together."

He squeezed me. "I hope you're right."

"When am I ever wrong?" I teased.

He kissed my forehead. "Never."

His phone rang. Parker grumbled as he sat up, and I moved to one side so he could get his phone from the end table. Because of the rescue, we couldn't ignore calls, especially this late at night.

He frowned. "It says it's likely spam."

We'd been getting a lot of robocalls at all times of the day and evening, and I'd made a practice of letting unknown calls go to voicemail. It was easier on my nerves to call someone right back if the call was legitimate, rather than get angry for picking it up in the first place. "Let it go to voicemail. If it's important, they'll leave a message, and you can call them right back."

Parker nodded and set the phone down. "Good idea. If I have to hear one more political recording, I might throw my cellphone into the woods." He set it down on the couch arm, as it rang twice more before clicking over.

"Well, that's that." Parker took me back in his arms as I scooted up onto his lap. His blue eyes crinkled at the corners as his generous mouth turned up in a smile. "I love you," he said with so much warmth it made my heart skitter.

"I love you," I said in return.

"I saw the way you looked for an escape route when Darren asked when we were getting hitched." He traced a finger over my lower lip. "But just so you know, I'm happy. I'm happy the way we are. I'll take you any way I can get you, Lily Mason."

I giggled nervously. Did Parker want to get married?

We'd talked about it before. There was no marriage or kids, other than the dogs, in our future, and we'd both seemed to be on the same page about it. I hoped he was teasing me, and I was reading too much into his playful banter. "You're my mate, Parker. And that is stronger than any bond a marriage could form. You're stuck with me for life."

He tucked one of my auburn curls back behind my ear. "And you're stuck with me." He leaned forward and pressed his lips to mine. "And that's the way I like it." He kissed me again as the gentle caresses of his fingers raised goosebumps on my skin and quickened my pulse. I pressed my body against his and threaded my fingers through the hair at the nape of his neck.

A big head with a cold nose burrowed into the space between my right thigh and Parker's arm. We broke from the kiss and laughed.

"How about we take this to the bedroom?" Parker asked.

"How about I take Elvis and Smooshie out first? That way we can take our time. No interruptions."

His phone vibrated. He frowned as he glanced down. "Voicemail," he said.

I patted his leg. "You check that, and I'll be right back." I hopped up from his lap. "Come on, you two." Elvis lifted his head from the bed, seeming almost reluctant to move from his warm, cozy place. I wiggled my brows at the loveable giant of a dog. "I'll let you chase me. Wanna chase?"

He stood up to his full four feet of height and woofed his acceptance of my challenge.

Parker shook his head, a smile on his face as the three of

us headed to the front door. My phone was on the charger, and the green light was blinking. I'd somehow missed a text from Ryan. I quickly checked. He found red phosphate on the rag, and Elinor's urine had tested positive for opioids and methamphetamines. The house had been used as a drug lab.

I slid on my boots and put on my coat, tucking the phone in my pocket. I'd call Ryan when I was done taking care of the dogs.

Smooshie's tail stopped wagging as I zipped my coat.

I shook my head. "I'm not going cougar tonight," I told her. I glanced back at Parker, who'd just put his phone to his ear. "I have other plans."

Smooshie whined. She much preferred me shedding clothes than putting them on. She loved to run through the woods with me when I was on my own four paws.

"I'm not changing my mind." I opened the door. "Come on now. Both of you out."

I didn't have to tell them twice. Elvis, with his long legs, loped out into the yard. Smooshie, with her shorter but more flexible legs, bounced around him like she was on a pogo stick. I chuckled. Elvis was such a tolerant soul. Even when Smooshie nudged his butt with her nose.

"You know where he's been," I told her. "Do your business, and we'll play a quick game of chase."

That perked Elvis up again. He was going on seven or eight now—it was hard to know for sure with rescues—and I worried some arthritis was settling in, so it always made me happy when he puppied–out.

Smooshie was already circling a spot in untouched

snow, while Elvis went to Parker's truck, hiked his leg, and peed on the tire.

Smooshie, on the other hand, was dragging her girly bits through the snow as she made a yellow path.

After, they both were beside me, ready to go. "Let's do it." I took off on a jog, with both pit bulls zooming past me at breakneck speeds. I could go that fast in my second nature, but as a bi-ped in boots, I was doing my best to keep up. I only slowed down when the dogs did, the cold air stealing my breath. Smooshie jumped up behind me, and I lost my balance, careening face-first into the snow. I flopped over onto my back, laughing hard as they both nudged and licked at my face.

"Stop it," I said. "I'm fine."

I sat up, my butt starting to feel the cold, and my phone rang.

"This is ridiculous." I retrieved it from my coat pocket. I expected another unknown number, but Mia's name flashed on the screen. I took the call. "Hi, Mia."

Her voice was shaky and full of panic. "Have you heard from Darren?"

"No," I told her. "Why? Is something wrong?"

"He didn't come home this evening. He always calls if he's going to be late. He dropped me off at home after we left Blaston today. Then he drove into town to pick up supplies for our shelter. He told me he'd be home by five. It's almost ten o'clock, Lily. I'm worried about him."

"He's not answering his phone?"

"He broke his phone and got that new one today. I didn't think to get the number. I mean, I thought he'd be home by now." She was crying. "I have a bad feeling in my gut."

"Did you call his friends?"

"I'm doing that now," she said, sounding angry and annoyed. Immediately, she was apologetic. "I'm sorry, Lily. I already called nearby hospitals. I would have called Parker, but I only had your number."

"It's okay," I said. "Did you call the police?" I got up and started back to the house, the dogs on my heels.

"Yes." Mia sniffled. "They took my information and said they'd send out an officer to check the roadways. In case he was in an unreported accident."

You didn't have to wait twenty-four hours to file a missing person's report in Missouri, but it didn't surprise me that they weren't willing to sound the alarms for an adult male. At least, they told her they would check out the roads. That was minimally something, considering the bad weather. The last place Darren had been was the abandoned house. "Maybe those cameras he'd set around that house in Blaston picked up something. Would he have gone over there?"

Mia paused. "Maybe." There was another pause. "I don't have a car, Lily. I tried Rowdy, and he's not answering either. Of course, he was out with that woman, so no telling what kind of occupied they are." Her frustration was palpable. "I can't go and search for him, and I feel like I'm losing my mind."

Parker was at the door. He had his winter gear on. I frowned. "Can I call you back?"

"Yes," Mia said. "Of course. I'm sorry for bothering you."

"You're not bothering me. I swear it. Give me a few minutes, and I'll get back to you."

"Okay."

I hung up as I reached Parker. "What's up?" I asked. "What was the voicemail about?"

"It was Darren. He said he saw something on the cameras at the abandoned house, and he wasn't sure what to do about it. He said he was heading over there. I tried to ring him back, but he's not answering."

"Crap. I just got a call from Mia. She's worried something's happened to him because he didn't come home." I sighed. "The good news is that the phone call you got was less than fifteen minutes ago. So, he's alive." I'd been a magnet for dead bodies since my arrival to Moonrise, and I wasn't looking to attract any more if I could help it.

"We should go and check on him," Parker said.

I called Mia and told her we were headed to Blaston to look for Darren. She was beyond grateful, and it took a minute or two to get her off the phone. While I hoped this was a matter of a forgetful husband with a misplaced phone, I couldn't shake the feeling that there was something sinister at work.

"I think we should call Bobby," I told Parker. There were some pretty nasty guys out there this afternoon, and I don't want to come up against them without a police presence." Bobby Morris was the acting sheriff for our county, and he was a friend.

"Are you going to call Nadine?" he asked.

"No way. It's late, and it's freezing outside. There's no

way I'm dragging my very pregnant friend into a potentially dangerous situation," I said defensively.

Parker held up his hands. "I agree. But we both know she's gonna be pissed about it."

I softened my tone. "She'll forgive me." I went inside and grabbed my purse. "Come on, kids," I told Smooshie and Elvis. "We're going for a ride."

CHAPTER 5

On the way to Blaston, the weather took a turn. Icy rain mixed with sleet slickened the roads. Parker put the truck in four-wheel drive, but even so, there were a few stop signs where we slid before halting. The micro-town had felt empty during the day but harmless. At night, with the inclement winter storm, the place took on a haunted feel. Of course, I grew up in a paranormal town where there was intrigue around every corner, so I'd been conditioned to be in a constant state of "waiting for the other shoe to drop."

"I'm worried," Parker said.

I rubbed my arms. "I'm sure he's okay," I told him with little conviction. I was worried too.

We'd tried several times to call Darren, but the phone calls went straight to a prerecorded message informing us that the user of this account had not set up voicemail for the phone.

"There's his truck," I said.

Our headlights illuminated the front of the abandoned house and Darren's truck parked in the driveway. According to the dually's sensors, the temperature outside had dropped a few more degrees.

Parker's mouth was set in a grim line as he turned off the engine.

Elvis stood up from the backseat and placed his head on Parker's shoulder. Parker's hand immediately cupped the giant dog's nose as he gave him a quick pet. Smooshie's tail whacked the back of my seat as she put her paws on the door handle and pressed her nose to the window's cold glass.

I reached back and patted her head. "Settle down," I told her. I didn't like the eeriness of the situation. "You get to stay in the truck with your bro."

Parker grabbed a heavy-duty flashlight, the kind with weight in it, from behind his seat. I retrieved a small one out of my purse.

The brisk wind mixed with icy rain cut across my face as we stepped out of Parker's pickup. Charcoal colored clouds shielded the moon, making it a particularly miserable night as the sleeting worsened.

When I'd called Bobby, he said he'd send a unit as soon as one was free, but it might be a little while since three units had been dispatched to a four-car pileup on the highway between Moonrise and Cape Girardeau. In other words, the opposite direction. I understood Bobby couldn't drop everything for a gut feeling, but he still apologized. With due diligence, he had warned me not to take any action until he could get some deputies to Blaston. But there was no possible way, other than physically tying Parker down, that I was keeping him out of the house. And there was no way I was letting him go in alone.

"Do you hear anything?" Parker asked in a whisper when we were standing outside the front door.

I concentrated, focusing my senses, but the clicking of sleet hitting the structure and ground outside made it hard for me to hear anything. "Nothing," I replied. "Too much ambient noise."

"Smell?" he asked.

I shook my head. Freezing cold temperatures had a tendency to hide organic odors.

"This is ridiculous. He's fine," Parker said, but his grip tightened on his flashlight. He was prepared for a fight. He opened the door. "Darren!" He barked the name as if it were an order. "You in here?"

No answer.

"Let's look around," I said. "He was wearing earbuds earlier and listening to loud music today. He couldn't hear me when I was calling for him."

We did a quick sweep of the ground floor, including the living area, two small bedrooms, a single bathroom, and a kitchen with broken cabinets and no appliances. It took all of about twenty seconds, then we went to the narrow hall with the basement door.

There was a sweet, iron scent I recognized well. "Blood," I hissed to Parker.

He nodded, his eyes widening in surprise. He flipped the flashlight around and held it high on the neck, ready to use it as a Billy club if the need arose.

Smooshie and Elvis barked excitedly.

Parker caught my expression. "What?" he mouthed.

"The dogs," I said quietly. "They're freaking out."

We cracked the basement door open, and I heard a scraping sound. Maybe Darren had fallen down the steps. "Something's moving down there," I told Parker. "He could be hurt."

"Darren," Parker hollered down the steps. "Are you down there?"

I heard heavy footfalls, slow, almost reluctant on the stairs. We both flashed our lights down the steps.

An enormous sense of relief washed through me as the beam landed on Darren's face. His expression was a combination of loss, bewilderment, and simmering rage. Then I saw it.

Blood. Lots of it. It was on his hands, his pants, and his shirt. Parker started to descend to his friend, but I stopped him. He looked at me, confusion apparent.

"Are you hurt?" I asked Darren.

He slowly shook his head.

"Whose blood is that?"

Darren's face crumpled, and he choked out a groan as he fell to the step above his feet and landed on his knees.

"It's okay," Parker said calmly. "We're going to help you. Just tell me what happened."

"Rowdy." Darren's voice was strained. "Rowdy's dead."

"Are you sure?" I asked. Sometimes, when emotions were involved, it was easy to jump to conclusions. Although, that much blood didn't indicate a happy outcome.

"Did he fall? Have you called an ambulance?" Parker asked.

"I dropped my phone, and it broke," Darren said.

"Again?" Goddess, this man needed a leash for his phones. "What happened?"

"I was scanning the video recordings when I stumbled across Rowdy and dropped it onto the concrete floor." His shoulders were hunched as he seated himself. He scratched his bald head, painting dark streaks onto his skin. "What am I going to tell Mia?"

I glanced at Parker. "I'm going downstairs to take a look," I said.

He nodded. "Careful."

"Hey, Darren, why don't you come up here with Parker. He can keep you company while I check on Rowdy. I have some medical training," I told him. Of course, it was with animals, not people, but I'd also grown up with an unhealthy obsession with medical textbooks. "Is there anyone else down there?" I wanted to make sure I wasn't walking into more trouble.

"No," Darren said. "Just Rowdy."

I heard sirens in the distance, but I didn't want to escalate the tense situation by pointing it out to Darren. I leaned close to Parker. "Cops are coming."

"How can you tell?"

"Sirens."

He frowned, and I knew why. Bobby wouldn't have sent his guys out here with full-on lights and sirens. Had someone called the cops with information that warranted immediate action? If so, who?

"Maybe it's for something else," Parker said.

"Probably." I touched his hand, and he looped his index finger with mine for a brief moment of comfort. "Help your friend."

Parker descended to Darren and helped him stand. I skirted past the two of them and into the basement. I moved the flashlight around until I saw the crumpled form lying next to the overturned kitty litter pan. I wrinkled my nose at the chemical, perfumed, and blood odors that filled the room.

I squatted next to Rowdy. Without his hat on, I could see he had similar blond hair to his sister Mia, with light curls past his ears. He wasn't wearing a jacket, and his shirt was slashed across the middle. There was a lot of blood. I palpated his wrist for a pulse.

Nothing.

I tried his neck, but it was the same. No pulse. He was still warm to touch but definitely dead. Considering the house was freezing, I knew it hadn't been very long since he'd died. I ran the beam of light over him from head to toe. His shirt pocket was ripped, his jeans had black marks on the shins, and his pristine pointy-toed cowboy boots were scuffed. I moved down for a closer look. There was some kind of white substance, definitely not snow, in the crevice between the sole and the leather on the right boot.

In the scattered kitty litter, I saw a glint of metal. I moved closer. It was a knife—military in style with a blackened handle. And there was blood on it.

It was time to call Bobby again.

There was a commotion upstairs. Yelling, shouting, a loud thump. Cripes. I sprinted up the stairs.

Gary Hall, a newish deputy, along with his partner Deb Morton, were putting Parker and Darren into handcuffs. I'd met them both before at Bobby Morris's victory party in November when he became our officially elected sheriff.

"Stop it!" I shouted. "What are you doing?"

"Ma'am," Deb shouted. "I'm going to need you to turn your flashlight off and step back."

The beam must have blinded her. I clicked the light off. "It's Lily Mason," I said hurriedly. "I'm the one who called Bobby Morris tonight. Why are you arresting them?"

"I know who you are, Ms. Mason, and we'll get this straightened out when everyone calms down," Deb said.

Gary shoved Darren against the wall. "We're responding to a 9-1-1 call about an assault with a deadly weapon, Ms. Mason."

"At this address?"

"Yes."

"Who made the call?"

"Mr. Ronald Dawson made the call."

"Who?"

"Rowdy," Darren groaned.

Gary nodded. "He said his brother-in-law was trying to kill him."

My stomach clenched as the situation went from pure awful to downright wretched.

CHAPTER 6

Red and blue flashing lights blinded me as I was ushered out of the house in front of the two deputies. They still had Parker and Darren in cuffs and refused to listen as both men proclaimed their innocence. At one point, Deputy Hall freed his taser when Darren protested too vigorously. "I'll put you on the ground, big man. Try me."

Parker's eyes shifted back and forth as if he couldn't decide whether to attack or run. I hoped to hell he did neither. He'd been in therapy for over a year now, and his PTSD from the war had been getting less frequent. I feared this incident would set him back in his recovery.

Deputy Morton opened the cruiser's back door and put Parker inside. Smooshie and Elvis lunged at the window of the pickup, Smooshie in the driver seat and Elvis in the back. Both were growling and barking, clearly scared by the commotion, the lights, and the noise. I started to jog toward the truck until Gary Hall yelled at me to stop. I turned, my heart racing as I saw he had a gun aimed at me.

"I need to take care of my dogs," I said.

"Put the weapon away," Deputy Morton said. She glared at her partner. "Everybody, calm down."

"Call the sheriff," I said. "Call him now. He knows Parker and I were on our way out here."

Smooshie scratched at the door, her whines incredibly heart-rending.

Deputy Morton nodded. "Take care of your dogs but keep them in the truck. I like dogs, and I don't want to have to shoot one of them if they decide to attack an officer."

"I don't want that either. They're frightened," I added. "Not aggressive. But I will keep them under control." I got inside the truck, and our two would-be protectors settled down.

Smooshie nudged my cheek, licked my face, then tried to put her head under my hand for reassurance. I obliged. I reached back and stroked Elvis' head, but his gaze never wavered from the cruiser imprisoning Parker.

I watched Morton cross the yard to her partner. She didn't get on her radio to call Bobby. Instead, she helped Deputy Hall subdue Darren and get him into their vehicle's backseat on the opposite side.

"Screw this," I hissed. I got my phone out and called Bobby. He picked up on the first ring.

"What's up, Lily? I still can't get anyone out to you. We had an emergency call."

"I know," I said tightly. "The call sent your deputies to our location."

"Damn it, Lily. What happened?"

"When Parker and I got here, it was quiet. We found his friend, but we also found the body of his friend's brother-in-law, Rowdy." I shook my head. "Ronald Dawson."

"Land sakes, you draw trouble like honey draws flies."

Like I need to be reminded. "Your deputies have arrested Parker and his friend Darren. Parker and I came together. Rowdy was dead before we got here. You have to call Deputy Morton and tell her to let him go." My voice caught as I thought about the idea of Parker spending one second in a cell. "You know he can't go through that again. He was only here to help a friend. He has nothing to do with whatever crime may or may not have taken place."

"Did you tell the officers that?"

"They won't listen. Your Deputy Hall is a hothead."

"He's new, but he's been doing a good job."

"He pulled his weapon on me," I said.

There was a moment of silence, then Bobby said, "Hang tight. I'll take care of it." He ended the call.

I swallowed the lump in my throat, thinking about how many ways the evening had gone wrong and how many ways it might have been much worse. Deputy Morton went into the house with her right hand on her holstered pistol and her left hand up at chin level, holding a flashlight.

She was finally going to examine the basement. Hall strode in my direction, and my adrenaline ratcheted up a notch. I had to fight to keep my cougar leashed. I was super-human, but I wasn't immortal. A bullet in the right place would kill me just like it would kill anyone else.

Besides, I'd been shot before, and I had no desire to repeat the experience.

Deputy Hall rapped on my window. I rolled it down a few inches.

"Get out of the car, Ms. Mason," he said. "I have some questions to ask you." He peered inside the truck, and his expression made me believe he was spoiling for a fight.

Smooshie and Elvis's energy matched my own as they paced and whined. "It's okay," I said to the animals, even though it felt anything but okay. "I'm not leaving the truck."

His bushy brows furrowed, and his eyes narrowed at me. "Get out of the truck *now*."

"Car 7, Deputy Hall, please call Sheriff Morris," a voice said from his radio. "He's on his way to your scene, and he wants to talk to you immediately."

Hall looked irritated, but he stepped away from the truck. "Don't move."

I hadn't planned on moving. "I'll be right here."

With the police lights still flashing, it made the yard easier to see. Luckily, the sleeting rain had slowed to a fine mist. Still, the slush on the ground made it impossible to distinguish any track, new or old. It was all sort of a mushy mess, and if the temperature didn't warm some, the ground would be covered in ice by morning.

I pulled my coat tighter around me and watched as Hall got off his phone then opened the cruiser door. He was talking to either Parker or Darren, maybe both, but I couldn't hear him over Smooshie and Elvis's worried whining and anxious panting. My relief was palpable when the deputy stepped back, and Parker slid his legs out and stood up. He turned around, and Hall took the handcuffs off him.

Parker rubbed his wrists as he walked toward the truck. I slid into the passenger seat as he opened the door and climbed inside. His face was red. Creases deepened between his eyes, and his lips thinned in an angry line. "That mother..." He shook his head. "I swear Lily, if he had shot you, I would have—" He banged his fists against the steering wheel. He didn't, or maybe he couldn't, look at me.

"I'm okay, Parker." I put my hand on his leg. "He didn't hurt me."

He swiveled his gaze to mine, his expression stark and haunted. "I can't lose you."

"I know," I told him, my voice calm and soothing. "I can't lose you either, so take a breath and stay with me."

Elvis put his head on Parker's shoulder. My guy took a deep breath then let it out. "That dude owes me sixty-five dollars for my next therapy session."

I chuckled. Not because I thought it was funny, but because Parker was making an effort to work through his anxiety with dark humor. I understood the impulse all too well. "I'm just glad he let you go. What did he say?"

"He confirmed with Darren that his brother-in-law was dead before we arrived. And then he told me to get out of the car."

I smirked. "I called Bobby. I hope Hall got a butt chewing."

Parker grimaced. "They wouldn't even let us explain when we were in the house. They took one look at Darren covered in blood and reacted. I'm not sure I can blame them. I might have had the same reaction if I'd been called to the scene of an assault, and there was that much blood." He scrubbed his face. "But damn, it freaked me out to get handcuffed again."

"I worried it might. But you seem...okay." I pressed my hand to his cheek, and he turned his face to softly kiss my palm.

"I'm getting better at pretending, then," he said.

Smooshie, who had her butt up against the passenger window, began to whimper.

"Oh," I said, making a face as the scent of Eau de Dog Farts filled the cab. "Oh, that's a bad one."

"Someone needs to take a nature break," Parker said as he rolled the window down a little more. "Wow, what are we feeding her?"

"I don't want to take her potties with Yosemite Sam out there ready to shoot or taser whatever moves." I heard sirens in the distance. "I think the cavalry is about to arrive." I tucked Smooshie's head under my arm. "Hold it together, girl. Just another minute or two." She did not. Another stink bomb choked the oxygen from the cab.

"Dang, Smoosh. That's straight-up chemical warfare." Parker rolled the window down even more and stuck his face out. "We survived the past half hour only to be taken out by gas."

I laughed and gagged at the same time. It was better than crying.

Two more cruisers arrived at that time, along with the coroner's van. Bobby Morris was in one of the vehicles, Deputies Joe O'Rourke and Liz Harris, who were both crime scene specialists, got out of the other. They both had duffle bags that they hauled toward the house. One of my other best friends, who happened to be a local doctor and the coroner, Reggie Crawford, got out of the coroner van. She was clad from head to toe in white winter gear. She looked ready for the slopes, not a crime scene, but I knew from past experience that Reggie was an expert in her field, and I'd seen her show up at other crime scenes in four-inch heels and a party dress. In her defense, she'd been on a date when she'd been called out to work. That said, I didn't have a single doubt about her ability to get the job done.

Bobby came to the open driver's side window. He was taller than Parker by at least three inches, and he had the most intense brown eyes. He peeked in at me. "You okay?"

"No," I told him honestly. "But I will be. Your deputy has an itchy trigger finger."

"He grew up in this area. Last week, he had a domestic call that went bad. A child had to be rushed to the hospital. I think he's overcompensating."

"He pulled a gun on Lily," Parker said coolly. "He needs to take a break before anyone else gets hurt because of a knee-jerk reaction."

"I hear you. I—" Bobby's nose crinkled. "Dang, is there a skunk in your truck?" Bobby asked as he took a full step back.

"It's Smooshie," I said.

"That last one might have been Elvis," Parker admitted.

"Can we take the dogs out for a potty break? Otherwise, it's going to get bad."

Bobby coughed as he backed up another step. "I can't imagine it worse than this."

"Then you've never cleaned up a giant pile of poop from the back of your vehicle."

Bobby smirked. "I certainly have. Only it wasn't from a dog."

Parker pulled a face.

"Eww," I said. "So gross."

"Uh-hm," Bobby agreed. "Take your dogs out. Stay out of the crime scene area. I'll talk to you two after, then you can go home. We'll take it from here."

Parker turned a serious look at Bobby. "Take it easy on Darren. He's a vet, and he has some PTSD issues. He says he found his brother-in-law already dead. I believe him."

Bobby frowned. "He's your friend, Parker. It's in our nature to believe our friends."

"You believed me," I said without any bitterness or sarcasm. "Just give Darren the benefit of the doubt, please."

"You know I'll be fair," Bobby said. "That's all I can promise."

CHAPTER 7

Even with a no-tug leash, Smooshie strained against her tether to check out all the commotion outside the pickup.

"We're here to poop, not explore," I chastised. My furry cuddle monkey had the curiosity of a cat. Elvis, of course, was a perfect gentleman, ignoring everything around us except Parker and doing his business.

There was a thicket of overgrown hedges down the far side of the house's yard and far enough away from the house that we wouldn't be adding any dog DNA for the crime techs to work around.

"I can't believe this is happening," Parker said.

"Why did they handcuff you?" I asked, now that we were out of earshot of the police. "It scared me to see you in restraints."

"Scared me too," he said. "They saw the blood on Darren, and Hall freaked out, got excited, and grabbed Darren. That's when Darren started shouting. I stepped in to help calm him down, and the next thing I know, I was in handcuffs, too."

"Goddess, what a mess." I shook my head. "You think Darren is innocent," I made it a statement, but there was a hint of a question in my tone. He'd told Bobby his army buddy couldn't do it, but under the right circumstances, anybody could be driven to kill, even if unintentional.

Parker had his head down, trying to avoid slick spots as we traversed the line of bushes. "I want to." His response told me everything I needed to know.

I'd had my phone on silent, so I checked it then put it back in my pocket. My stomach hurt as anxiety squeezed the air from my lungs. "Mia's texted me a dozen times wanting to know if we've found Darren yet."

"We should call her."

"We should ask Bobby first. He might want to be the one to tell Mia that her brother has died."

Parker tensed as he jammed his free hand in his pocket. "I forgot Rowdy was her brother."

"Do you know her well?" I asked.

"Not at all," Parker said. "I haven't met her."

Mia had called me when she couldn't find Darren, not Parker. But earlier in the day, she'd acted like Parker had made plans for dinner on Friday. Or maybe that had been Darren. "Did Darren invite you to dinner this Friday?"

Parker shook his head. "Just the open invitation. Why?"

"Mia firmed up plans for Friday night this afternoon, and it felt like a done deal, so I agreed."

"Hm," Parker grunted. "Weird. Darren said she's a real take-charge gal. He liked that about her right away." He stopped as Elvis found a hollowed-out area between the hedges to squat and looked at me meaningfully.

"Are you trying to tell me that I'm bossy?"

He gave me a quick kiss. "Nope. Not bossy, just the boss."

I glanced at Smooshie, who had peed five times, once in every place she caught a scent, but hadn't pooped, yet. "You better get to gettin', missy, or you're going to be holding it until we get back home."

Parker quirked a half-grin at me. "See. Totally the boss."

"Stop." I swatted him away. "Hurry up, Smoosh."

Smooshie panted, playfully growled, and wagged her tail as if to say, *I go when I gotta go, cougar. Deal with it.* Suddenly her stance went rigid, her back straight, tail up, and ears perked.

"Squirrel," Parker said.

"Probably," I agreed. I scratched her ears. She ducked away from my hand, still on full alert. I stretched my own senses and heard a rustling sound. I grasped Parker's sleeve and pointed to my ears. I handed him Smooshie's leash and squatted down to take a look.

Smooshie barked a sharp warning, and a small rabbit jumped from the bushes and hopped as fast as it could toward the backyard. Smooshie charged about the same time Parker was adjusting his hold, and the next thing I knew, she was in a full sprint.

Parker cursed a few choice words that I was thinking as I raced, my winter boots grabbing the wet snow, to stop Smooshie from getting away.

"Come back here," I snapped. There wasn't anyone in the backyard, so I risked using my supernatural reflexes and leaped the fifteen foot divide between Smooshie and myself and caught her leash, landing in a crouch near her. Just as suddenly as she'd taken off, she came to an abrupt stop and was sniffing and pawing at the ground.

I scanned the area to make sure I hadn't been seen, and I reeled Smooshie in. "You are going to be the end of me, girl. You know that, right?"

She licked my face.

"That's what I thought." She turned her attention again back to where she'd been digging. "What do you have there?"

There was a small, plastic white box with a dark circle on the front. One of Darren's cameras. What was it doing out here in the yard? The side of it was cracked as if someone had stomped on it.

Even so, I chastised myself for forgetting about the cameras. If Rowdy's death had been caught on video, it could exonerate Darren.

Or convict him.

Either way, it would get to the truth of the matter. The cameras were battery operated and only recorded when they detected movement, so there was no cord to mess with. I had more dog refuse bags in my coat, so I used one to pluck the camera from the ground. I wouldn't be adding my prints.

"You okay?" Parker called out.

"Yep. Good," I answered. I gave Smooshie another head scritch. She pranced as we crossed the backyard to where Parker and Elvis waited. Her earlier sprint must have greased her plumbing because she finally did three quick turns, then had at it.

"What you got there?" Parker asked.

"It's one of Darren's motion cameras. Smooshie found it half-buried in the yard."

I could see him kicking himself mentally the same way I had.

"Yeah," I agreed. "I can't believe we forgot about the cameras."

"We better tell Bobby," he said.

"After we get these two back in the truck."

Parker nudged me with his shoulder. "Good plan."

"Where did you find this?" Deputy Morton asked. Bobby had tasked her with getting our statement after Deputy Harris, the female crime tech, took the camera from me.

"The backyard," I said.

"And why did you go in the backyard?"

I cast a baleful glance back to the dually where we'd dropped the fur kids. "My dog took off after a rabbit but got sidetracked when she stumbled upon the camera in the backyard."

Her expression remained suspicious. "You say there are several of these cameras on the property."

"Six of them. Darren could give you more information on their whereabouts, but he said he put two outside and four inside, including down in the basement."

She stopped taking notes and cast a glance at the other officers. "Thanks, Ms. Mason. I better go tell the team."

Reggie came out of the house. She looked weary. Exhausted. I understood. Death took its toll. She handed off her bag to Harris, and with her feet still bootied, she joined me in the yard. "Hey, Lils." She shook her head. "Why am I not surprised to see you here?"

"I'm sure lots of crimes happen without me being around," I said flatly.

"Sure. Robberies, kidnapping, car theft..." She raised her brow at me. "Just not murder." I'd known Reggie for a few years now, and we'd been the best of friends since our first case together when Smooshie had found a mummified foot in the wall of my house during the renovation. She and her daughter had moved from Kansas City to Moonrise to get away from a toxic ex–husband, and she, Nadine, and I had been thick as thieves ever since. She was part of the handful of friends who knew the truth about Buzz and me being shifters. And soon, she would be Parker's new stepmom.

She'd felt like family for a long time, but I was still thrilled to have one more tie.

"So, you think it's murder?"

"The only thing I'm certain of is that Mr. Dawson's death wasn't an accident." She looked around to make certain she couldn't be overheard. "I can't really talk about it right now. But, you know, maybe over lunch tomorrow with Nadine..."

A slip of a smile tugged at my lips. "You're on."

"Great. Now, I've got to get the body back to the morgue. I'm going to do a preliminary exam tonight."

I looked over her white winter pants and coat with a

puffy hood. "Why are you dressed like you're going to a resort?"

"Greer and I are going up to Hidden Valley for a ski weekend," she explained.

"Tonight?"

"No, smarty pants. I bought the outfit online, and it came in the mail today. And," she added. "It is really freaking cold outside, and this ski suit is really freaking warm."

I scoffed. "Warm enough, you were willing to get blood on it to stay warm?"

"It wasn't that expensive," she said. "I have already put in an order for another one in eggplant purple."

"Pretty."

"Shut up." She rolled her eyes. "I've got to get back to work. See you tomorrow?"

"Absolutely."

I joined Parker and Bobby by the cruiser, holding Darren. Neither of them looked happy.

"What's wrong?" I asked, then felt like an idiot. At the moment, there wasn't a whole lot of right.

"The cameras are missing," Parker said.

Bobby gave him a terse stare.

"Did Darren take them down?" I asked.

Bobby sucked his teeth. "He says not. And since his phone is busted up, we can't corroborate any of his story."

"If he's under arrest, he shouldn't be talking to you at all."

"He had his rights read to him," Bobby said. "And he hasn't asked for a lawyer."

Parker knocked on the door window. Darren didn't look up at him. "Lawyer," Parker said loudly.

"That's enough," Bobby said. "Why don't you two head home? You can come by in the morning to make an official statement."

"What about Darren's wife?" I asked. "She's worried sick and has been trying to reach me for the past hour. The victim is her brother."

Bobby took his hat off and scratched his short curls. "It's a sticky one. Was Ronald Dawson married?"

I shook my head. "He has a girlfriend, though. They were in Moonrise earlier to shop and eat. At least, that's where they said they were going." I didn't mention Nadine knew him from high school. If she thought her connection to Rowdy was pertinent to the investigation, she would tell Bobby herself. "I can't remember the girlfriend's name, but Darren or Mia could tell you. She drives a fancy sports car." I don't know why I added the last part. I guess because she didn't seem to be the kind of woman to drive a muscle car.

"I'll get her name from the sister," Bobby said.

"Do you want company when you talk to her?" I couldn't help but think about my own losses and how hard this would be for Mia, even if her husband was innocent. "I lost my only brother a few years back. I know how difficult it can be."

The lines at the corners of Bobby's eyes softened. "I wish I could bring you along, Lily. But I'm under a microscope now that I'm the actual sheriff." He glanced at his deputies as they trekked back and forth between the house and the coroner's van. "I have to be more careful about following the rules because I have more to lose now."

I knew Bobby had two small boys at home, and his wife, Carly, was an English adjunct at the college. I knew from Ryan that adjuncts didn't get paid much, so I imagined the bump in pay helped quite a bit.

I didn't want to make trouble for him. "I'll call her tomorrow." I almost laughed at his evident relief. "I'm not that bad."

Bobby didn't comment.

Parker put his arm around me. "Are we free to go?" he asked Bobby.

The man nodded. "Don't forget to come in tomorrow and make a statement."

"We won't forget," I assured him. Though, I really was tired of dealing with death. My whole life felt as if I just stumbled upon one body after another. "Even if I wanted to."

CHAPTER 8

At eight o'clock in the morning, there were six vehicles parked in the client parking lot at Petry's Pet Clinic. Tuesdays and Saturdays were busy mornings because Ryan did surgery on Mondays and Fridays, with a lot of the patients overnighting for observation.

I'd forgotten about his message last night—the one about the red phosphorous. I needed to get the scrap of cloth back from Ryan and give it to Bobby. I wasn't sure if it would be helpful to the investigation, but I didn't want to hold evidence that might prove someone else was in that basement other than Darren. He'd said he didn't kill Rowdy. I would give him the benefit of the doubt. Innocent until proven guilty was the ideal, but it wasn't always how it was handled. After all, they'd arrested Parker and my uncle, both with purely circumstantial evidence, and the sheriff had tried to direct the evidence to assure their convictions. Of course, that had been Sheriff Avery, who, it turned out, was not above lies and corruption.

I had to believe Bobby was above railroading suspects. At least, I hoped so.

Either way, getting the probably drug-related rag to the police was a priority. Parker and I were meeting after lunch to give our statements, and I would hand it over then.

At reception, Abby told me Ryan was back in the recovery kennels checking on patients. I found him with an overweight Pomeranian who'd had six teeth pulled because her gums had become infected due to misalignment and poor hygiene. It was pretty major, but the little fluff-ball would be feeling much better in a few days.

My phone beeped. I pulled it from my scrub pocket and glanced at the screen, worried it might be from Mia. She hadn't texted since last night. I could only assume it was because Bobby had already told her everything. I'd call later and offer my sympathies and see if there was anything I could do for her. Finding out her brother was dead and her husband arrested was a double blow. I hope she had the support she needed.

My heart ached for Mia and for my own loss. My brother Danny had been in and out of trouble since his teens with drugs and other illegal activities. I found out after he died that he'd been sober for six months. I spent so much time his last two years pushing him away, keeping him at an emotional distance, that I hadn't even realized he was trying to fix his life. My knowledge wouldn't have saved Danny. I know this. But I still blamed myself for not being able to make a more comfortable life for him. Our parents died my senior year of high school, and I'd had to drop out to support the two of us. Danny had been seven years old at the time, and I'd been both sister and mother from then on. It's hard to be a parent and friend, and I never could strike the right balance between us.

But the message wasn't from Mia. It was from Nadine, and she had eight words for me. *Oh, Lily. You have some 'splainin' to do.*

The 'splainin' would have to wait until lunch. *See you at Cat's Meow at 12:10. Reggie is meeting us. Will explain then,* I sent back.

She sent me a full row of poop emojis as a reply. I pocketed my phone.

"How are my favorite lovebirds?" I asked Ryan after he placed the Pomeranian back in the kennel.

"They're doing pretty good this morning," he said. "I went ahead and put Eleanor on some Fluoxetine, and it helped her rest last night."

"For the methamphetamines?" I'd learned in my pharmacology class that Fluoxetine was generic for Prozac, a commonly used medication for dogs with significant anxiety.

Ryan nodded his head. "I went ahead and gave her a dose of naloxone, an opioid inhibitor, as well. That will help her with any withdrawals she might be experiencing. She's not nearly as anxious as she was when she came in two days ago. I think she was going through withdrawal from being exposed to methamphetamines and opioids."

I was furious about what had happened to Edward and Elinor. Although working with Parker the past few years at the rescue, I'd learned that there were some people capable of all manner of horrendous acts.

Ryan checked the belly bandages of a cat that had been neutered the day before. "The good news is that Edward, other than being underweight, is no worse for wear. I don't think he's had near the exposure to the meth lab that Elinor did."

"Maybe he's a fairly new addition," I said.

"Possibly," Ryan said. "I heard you had some excitement last night."

"What exactly did you hear?"

"That you stumbled onto another body."

"Not true," I stated emphatically. "Someone else did the stumbling." I narrowed my gaze at him. "And how in the world did you find out so fast? It's a little after eight in the morning, and we didn't even leave the scene until close to midnight."

"News travels fast around here," he said.

"This is more than fast. It's light speed."

Abby poked her head back. "Dr. Petry, could you come up front."

Ryan nodded to her. "Be there in a sec." To me, he said, "We're not done with this conversation."

"I'm going to go check on Elinor and Edward before I get started this morning."

"Absolutely," he said. "I think that they're lonely. They'll be glad for the company."

When I entered the isolation room, Eleanor and Edward were cuddled up on their raised bed. Eleanor had her head flopped across Edward's neck, and when I opened the door to the kennel, both their tails started wagging. It made me happy to see that they weren't wholly distrustful of people.

"Hey, guys. How're you doing?" I sat down, cross-legged, on the floor in front of them and let them make the first move.

They both stood up and came over, but Edward was the first to let me pet him. "Such a sweet boy," I crooned.

Once Edward got the lovin's, Elinor wasn't far behind. She wasn't shaking anymore. That was a step in the right direction. Gosh, they were lovely babies. The two were going to make some family very happy. I could see right away that they would be easy to get along with. And the fact that they were bonded meant that they were likely tolerant of other dogs. Of course, the proof of that still remained to be seen.

I went to the counter to get a couple of treats from the jar, and both Elinor and Edward sat at my feet. They were so much more patient than Smooshie as they waited for the nibbles coming their way. They took the offered goodies and returned to the large kennel when I screwed the lid down on the jar. Had they been trained? There was so much we didn't know about the dogs we rescued, but it didn't stop me from wondering.

"I'll check in on you two later." I closed the kennel door and latched it. "I'm happy to see you both doing so well. We'll find you a home real soon."

When I stepped out of the room, Kelly was carrying a small beagle, one that I hadn't seen before, out of the recovery room.

"This is Precious," she said. "Poor little thing tore her toenail."

Precious had a pink bandage wrapped around her front paw. "Ouch."

"You're telling me. Ryan had to put in a couple of stitches." She scratched the beagle's belly, then gave her a kiss on the head. "All good now and ready to go home."

"Excellent news."

Kelly gave me an odd look. "I'm surprised you're at work today."

"Why? I work half-days every Tuesday."

"I heard about last night. That must have been awful finding a body like that."

How in the world had everyone heard about last night? "I didn't exactly find it. It was already found. How did you hear about it?" My irritation created a more robust effect with my truth ju-ju.

"Deb told me." Her face was full of consternation. "I wasn't supposed to say that."

My jaw dropped. I closed it. "Deputy Deb Morton? Did she call you?"

"She came over. We've been...seeing each other for a couple of months now." Kelly looked horrified as the words left her mouth, and I felt terrible about forcing the truth from her. But obviously, she'd secretly wanted someone to know. I couldn't make anyone tell me a truth they never wanted unmasked in the first place.

"Oh." I blinked. "I'm glad you're seeing someone. If she makes you happy, that's all that matters."

"Thanks," she said. Then I realized I'd read her horror wrong. "I don't care if anyone knows, Lily. I've been out to my family and close friends for a while now."

That was surprising news. She hadn't once mentioned it to me, but I understood. We were friendly co-workers, not friends. At least not the kind of friends who shared secrets, and my secrets were a matter of survival.

"Deb isn't out yet, and she doesn't want her work to know she's a lesbian." Kelly looked at me. "I'd appreciate it if you'd keep that to yourself."

"It's in the vault."

Kelly scratched the beagle behind the ear. "You missed your calling as a therapist, Lily. You're always so easy to talk to." She rubbed Precious under the chin. "I better get this one to her momma."

I wanted to ask her more about Deputy Morton, but I'd already abused my power enough. There was something off about Morton's behavior last night. At first, I'd thought it was because her partner was so jumpy, but maybe there was something else I wasn't seeing. Or, perhaps, seeing Rowdy, dead and bloody, had taken a toll. I'd have to ask Nadine what she knew about Morton.

Ryan popped his head out from behind the exam room door. "Hey, Lils, come help keep a St. Bernard calm while I draw some blood."

I gave him a quick nod. "Coming."

CHAPTER 9

I drove past Parker's old home on the way to The Cat's Meow Cafe. It had changed significantly since he'd moved in with me onto our twelve-acre property northeast of town. For one, the new owners had replaced the old vinyl siding and re-shingled the roof on the house. The backyard, which used to have a chain-link fence around the perimeter, now had a five-foot-high privacy fence. I wondered what they'd done to the apartment over the garage, the one I'd lived in when I first arrived in town. Probably turned it into a home office or something. The biggest change was to the shelter. They'd gotten commercial zoning, and had turned the space into a grooming business for cats and dogs call, the Claw and Paw Salon.

I was glad the house had gone to such a lovely couple, but I couldn't help but feel a mild sense of loss. I was on a new and more exciting path, but I would forever be thankful for the last chapter in my life.

The Cat's Meow Cafe, my Uncle Buzz's diner, was only a

few blocks away. I'd walked to it from Greer's Rusty Wrench auto shop the very first day I'd driven into Moonrise, Missouri. My poor truck had coughed and sputtered then died in Greer's parking lot. It was a day that changed my life forever. I'd met Smooshie and Parker, and the search for my last remaining relative had turned Moonrise into a place I called home.

The parking lot at The Cat's Meow was packed, as usual for a weekday lunch rush. It was common knowledge that Buzz had the best burgers in town. I slid into a spot close to Reggie's ivory Lexus. Nadine's sheriff's vehicle was parked in the grass around the side of the diner. Good. They were both here already.

There was a sharp ding as I opened the glass door. Nadine and Reggie were sitting in the first of six booths situated along the wall. There were four tables and no empty seats to be had. Even the counter seating had a butt on every stool. The interior décor hadn't changed much over the years. It was still rustic country with orange tabby kitsch and trinkets everywhere. I smiled when I saw two elderly women, one with snowball-white hair, the other with dyed purple, in the last booth. The Dixon sisters, Opal and Pearl, were regulars, and Buzz always reserved the booth at the end for them.

I waved at Nadine and Reggie but slipped past them to give Opal and Pearl hugs.

"Oooo-wee," Pearl said. "Look what the cat dragged in."

They had no idea I was a werecougar, but I had decided a few months back that at some point in time, I would tell them. If there was one thing I knew for sure, it was that the Dixon sisters knew how to keep a secret.

"Hey, Pearl. Looking good. I like the new hair color."

"It's passion purple," she said. "My man says it makes me look spicy."

I'd accidentally walked in on Pearl and her man, aka Bob Tolliver, having sex on a shower chair this past summer. I didn't need any more reminders of her spiciness. "How is Bob?" I asked.

Opal rolled her eyes. "Intrusive."

Pearl ignored her sister. "Frisky as ever." She gave her hair a quick pat. "Where's your sexy hunka hot pants?"

Opal shook her head. "Pearl, you are getting out of hand."

"That's what he said," she cackled.

Opal sighed. "That doesn't even make sense, you old fool." She looked at me. "Don't mind Pearl. She's addled from being oversexed."

I laughed. The sisters bickered constantly, but I knew these two would die for each other. And, well, they would also kill for each other. They'd ended up in Moonrise as a result of Opal killing Pearl's abusive husband. He'd been a money launderer for a mob boss in Vegas. They'd taken all his ill-gotten cash from his safe and fled to Missouri. They changed their names to Pearl and Opal Dixon, and from that day forward, they'd never looked back.

"Do you want to join us?" Pearl invited.

"Can't today, ladies. I'm meeting with Reggie and Nadine. Another time, though."

Opal nodded. "There's always a seat at our table for our favorite sleuth."

I'd investigated the apparent suicide of the nurse who'd been taking care of Opal when she'd broken her hip over the summer. Opal had been convinced the young woman would not have taken her own life, and she'd been right. With a little help from my friends, we'd managed to catch the murderer and get justice for the nurse's family.

Pearl glanced at me. "Opal may need to hire you again. Lately, she can't find her butt with two hands."

"Is her butt missing?"

Opal snorted. "For about a decade now. It's hell getting old, kiddo. Your belly gets bigger, and your butt disappears."

Opal and Pearl used to be chorus girls, and they were both still in great shape for being in their late seventies. "I'll keep an eye out for it," I said with all seriousness, then giggled.

"Speaking of dead bodies," Opal said with the worst transition in the history of transitions. "I heard you found that Rowdy kid last night."

"Just tragic," Pearl added.

"How does everyone know this?" I asked. Surely, Deb Morton wasn't dating Opal, too.

"Word gets around, Lily. And information is currency. The more you know, the more you're worth," Pearl said.

Pearl, at one point, was delivering poison pen notes to folks in town. She kept her accusations vague enough that many guilty people had worried someone knew about their transgressions. I'd been one of the people Pearl had targeted, and for a hot minute, I'd thought my life in Moonrise was over. It turned out Pearl had been bored. She was more interested in seeing folks react to her notes than following through with blackmail.

"Well, to add to your piggy bank, I didn't stumble, trip, or find Rowdy. I showed up after he was discovered."

"That poor sister of his. She must be in a state. She raised him, you know. Their parents died in a house fire when Mia was twenty and Rowdy was fourteen. That girl put her life on hold to take care of him so he wouldn't go into foster care."

My stomach clenched. Mia and Rowdy's story reminded me too much of my own. "I didn't know," I said.

Opal gave me a sympathetic nod. She knew enough of my story to draw the parallel. "It was over a decade ago. Long before you or even Buzz arrived in town."

Buzz had been around Moonrise for nine years now, but he was still regarded by some of the old-timers as an outsider.

Finding Buzz had been a lifeline for me after Danny died. I hoped Mia had someone she could turn to right now. Especially since her husband might be the reason her brother was dead. "Did they have any other family?"

"Nope, just each other," Opal said.

"Poor Mia."

The sisters nodded their agreement.

I tapped on the table. "It's good seeing you both. We'll talk soon."

"If you decide to investigate," Pearl said. "We want in on the action. We might not have two good hips between us, but we have four excellent ears and fair to middling eyes."

"Mine is better than fair since my cataract surgery," Opal insisted. "But Pearl's right. If we hear anything of note, we'll let you know."

"Thanks. Just don't go putting yourself in danger." I gave Opal a kiss on the cheek and then her sister. "I've lost enough family already."

Leon carried a tray of food to Nadine and Reggie's booth.

I moved quickly, narrowly avoiding Laura Hambly's baby bag that she'd slid into the aisle, to beat Leon to the table. I slid in next to Reggie, elated with my small victory. I never ordered anymore. Instead, I let Buzz surprise me. Right now, everything sounded good. I was starved.

Reggie slid a drink to me. "There's your soda. I thought the ice was going to melt before you got here."

I took a deep sip from the straw. "Aww," I said with satisfaction. "Perfect."

"Who's got the bacon cheeseburger with pickle relish and peanut butter with a side of sweet potato fries and ranch dressing?" Leon asked.

Nadine raised her hand. "That'd be me." She gave Reggie and me a look that dared us to say something as Leon set the food down in front of her.

"And the BLT with avocado on whole wheat with a side of steamed broccoli?" he asked.

Nadine and I stared at Reggie.

"What?" She took the offered plate. "I want to lose a few pounds before our trip."

"You are a stick, woman," Nadine chided. She patted her

belly. "Unlike me." She was wearing a brown, maternity, uniform shirt, or what she liked to call the turd tent.

"And lastly," he said as he placed food in front of me, "two double deluxe bacon cheeseburgers, a side of steak fries, a chocolate shake, and fried cheese curds with ranch dressing."

I wiggled my brows. "Get in my belly!"

Nadine and Reggie laughed. They were amused, and I thought, secretly jealous of my voracious appetite, but Leon shook his head. He didn't ask me where I put it, and for that, he had my respect.

Giddy as a werekitty on her first hunt, I clapped my hands and did a little chair dance. "Tell Buzz he did good."

Leon grinned. "Will do, Lily."

Nadine took a huge bite of her burger and sighed. "Oh, so delicious."

I looked at her. "You're not nauseated?"

She cracked a smile, and with a mouth full of bread and beef, she said, "Nope."

"Oh, that's so good to hear," Reggie said. "I was afraid the medicine wouldn't work."

"What medicine?" I asked as I ate a hot cheese curd, then had to breathe real fast through my mouth to cool it down.

"Unisom and B six," Reggie answered.

"A sleep medicine and a vitamin?"

Nadine nodded as she took another bite. This time she swallowed before answering. "That's what I said. But I feel better today than I have in months."

"Wonderful. I can't tell you how worried I've been."

"Mmm–hmm," she hummed sourly. "Worried enough to not call me when you drove out the Blaston last night?"

"Let me have it, but I wouldn't have done it any differently. I love you, and that means I'm going to make decisions to protect you, even when you don't like it."

"I'm the cop, Lily."

"And I have other advantages," I pressed.

She rolled her eyes. "Fair. But still, you should have called me."

"Probably," I admitted. I turned to Reggie, who had eaten half her sandwich already, and asked in a hushed voice so the tables around us wouldn't hear, "Did you find anything interesting when you examined Rowdy?"

"Funny enough," she said in the same quiet register, "I did."

Nadine craned forward. "Well, don't leave us hanging, Reg."

"The slice across his stomach isn't the cause of death."

I leaned in closer. "Well?"

"Ronald Dawson choked to death on twenty-two one-dollar bills."

CHAPTER 10

"Wait...what?" Nadine put her burger down. "Was he choked by a stripper?"

"How do you choke on dollar bills?" I asked.

"Not easily. The money was crumpled, and the lining of his throat scratched and bloody. Someone shoved them down his throat so fast and with so much force he couldn't swallow them."

The horror of Rowdy's last moments struck me. This wasn't an accident or a crime of passion. Whoever had killed Rowdy had done the deed deliberately and with enough calculation, that he or she continued the process until he was dead.

"Did it take all twenty–two wads to kill him?" I asked.

Reggie raised a dark brow. "I'd say his oxygen supply was completely blocked off by bill number fourteen or fifteen, but whoever killed him didn't stop until the bills were past his epiglottis and into his tracheal tube."

"Hmm. Why not stop when he was dead? And why

twenty-two one-dollar bills? Why not twenty? Or twenty-four?"

"I'm guessing twenty-two was significant to the killer," surmised Reggie.

"Ugh." Nadine pushed her plate aside. "There has to be an easier way to take someone out."

"There are hundreds of easier ways to murder someone, and between the three of us, we could probably come up with most of them, but Ronald Dawson was killed with this method. Choked by less money than it would take to buy all three of our lunches." She glanced at my food. "Well, maybe not Lily's."

"Buzz isn't going to charge us," I said. He never did. Lunch was always on the house for the three of us. I was pretty sure he didn't charge the Dixon sisters either.

"Not the point," Reggie countered.

"I'm not discounting the stripper angle," Nadine said. "Did you check the bills for coconut oil and body glitter?"

Reggie smirked. "I'll look into that."

"Wow." I sat back for a moment to digest this information. Darren had been covered in blood, including both his hands. "I don't recall any blood on Rowdy's face. At least, nothing significant. Did you?"

My friend tugged at the short hairs at the nape of her neck. "There wasn't much." She shook her head. "No bloody handprints, if that's what you mean."

"Why slash him across the stomach if you were going to suffocate him with money?" It didn't make sense for Darren to summarily choke the life out of his brother-in-law with wads of cash, only to slash his stomach after and then put his hands all over the blood. And if Rowdy was already dead when he got cut, would he have had bled that much? "Was he sliced up before or after he died?"

"The laceration to his stomach probably happened before he died, but given the amount of blood and damage, it wasn't too long before he choked to death. However, the blade never penetrated the muscle wall," Reggie answered. "So maybe it was an attempt at torture, or the killer wanted to disable him enough to shove cash down Rowdy's throat."

"You mean, he wanted him alive long enough to know he was being murdered," said Nadine, horrified.

I glanced at Nadine, who looked sallow in the cheeks. "Darren had Rowdy's blood on his hands and clothing when we got there. Why would he slash his brother-in-law, then stuff money down his throat, then fingerpaint in his blood afterward? He'd have to be completely incompetent."

"Maybe he is," Nadine said. "I talked to Gary Hall this morning, the arresting officer, and he said that Darren admitted Rowdy's death was his fault."

"You mean the same Gary Hall who pulled his weapon on me last night and threatened to shoot me?"

Nadine and Reggie both let out audible gasps.

"That's right," I said. "That guy is as jumpy as a cricket, but dangerous, since, you know, he carries a loaded weapon."

Anger lines deepened on Nadine's forehead. "I'm going to take a certain rookie on a long walk off a short pier," she said. "What in the hell was he thinking?"

I shook my head. "It was total chaos. If Deputy Morton hadn't stepped in, I'm not sure what would've happened."

Nadine nodded. "Deb's one of the good ones."

I was still reserving judgment on Deb Morton at this point. She'd told Kelly about the murder, and Kelly had come to work and told everyone else. That kind of loose-lipped talk could get her fired. I didn't tell Nadine because I'd have to explain how and why Deb had told Kelly, and I made it a point not to out folks who didn't want to be outed.

Buzz came out of the kitchen, wiping his hands on a clean dishtowel as he walked in our direction. And he was completely clean-shaven. Beard gone. "Lunch okay?"

I dropped my fry as I stared at a face I hadn't seen in several years. I swallowed the knot in my throat as I stared up at the spitting image of my brother Danny. Or, what Danny might have looked like given another fifty years and some extra sun on his cheeks and forehead.

"I..." I couldn't formulate words.

"What did you do?" Nadine asked, her eyes wide. The entire cafe grew quiet as more people noticed the change in Buzz's appearance.

He shrugged, ignoring everyone but Nadine. "I wanted you to know that I heard you."

"By shaving off your beard?" She took a sip of her tea. "Color me surprised. You look so...wow. So young."

"You look like Danny," I said with a croak.

"I didn't mean to upset you. Either of you." Buzz glanced back and forth from Nadine to me, his frown deepening. "It'll grow back."

"It's all right." I fought to hold back the tears threatening to spill down my cheeks. "It just caught me off guard." In a way, it was kind of nice. I'd always thought Buzz looked a lot like my dad, but now I could see that my brother, who'd been given Buzz's birth name of Daniel, looked more like our uncle. It felt as if I were seeing a ghost.

"I feel like I'm looking at a stranger," Nadine said. "I've known you for years, and I've never seen you without at least an inch of facial hair."

"When you yelled that my face stank last night, I decided to surprise you. I had to stop by Walmart this morning and get some supplies." His brow furrowed as he scratched his clean-shaven chin. "I'll admit I might not have thought it through."

"I think you look...handsome," Reggie said.

"Pretty," Nadine corrected. "I think the word you're looking for is pretty. Like one of those high fashion male models. The symmetry in your bone structure is unbelievable."

He rubbed his cheeks. "It feels weird. I haven't seen my face like this in over thirty years."

That made sense. It was easier to hide the fact that your face barely aged behind a beard.

Nadine scooted from the booth and slid her hands behind his neck. She stared up at Buzz for a few seconds, then pressed her lips to his in a kiss that started innocently enough but quickly deepened.

I heard a few nervous throat clearings, a soft cough, and someone muttered, "get a room."

When they stopped kissing, Nadine gazed up at Buzz. "It feels like I'm cheating on you."

He chuckled and tapped his knuckles against her chin. "Hold that thought for later tonight."

"Sake's alive," I heard Pearl say with a hissing breath. "That one's going in the old spank bank."

Buzz's grin widened, the dark circles under his eyes easing, as he cast a glance back to the elderly sisters and gave Pearl a wink. "I better get back to work." He looked around the room at all the diners and added, "Get a good look, because much like Jupiter aligning with Saturn, this is an event that won't be coming back around in your lifetime."

There was a titter of laughs as conversations in The Cat's Meow Cafe started back up again.

He kissed Nadine again. "I love you," he said. "And I'd shave my entire body if it meant making you happy."

"I love you, too." She gave him a hug. "Please don't shave anything else."

He chuckled and gave her a peck on the forehead. "Not a single hair," he replied before letting her go and heading back into the kitchen.

"Well, that was unexpected," Reggie said.

"You're telling me." Nadine sat back down. "I'm still in shock." They both looked at me. "Are you okay?" Nadine asked.

I shook my head, then nodded. "Yes. Fine." Rowdy's death and Buzz's face reveal stirred up a bunch of past emotions, regrets, and unresolved grief inside me. "It was a surprise, is all."

"You're telling me." Nadine snorted. "I feel like I'm in

high school again, only the captain of the football team is the father of my babies."

Reggie choked back a laugh. "Wasn't Parker the captain of your football team? Did you have a lot of fantasies about him?"

I giggled. "Yes, Nadine, please tell us all about your teenage dreams."

Nadine rolled her eyes. "I only have fantasies for one guy, beard or no beard."

"Does this sound like a case of protesting too much?" Reggie asked me.

"Why, I think you might be right, Dr. Crawford."

"You're both terrible human beings."

Reggie nudged my shoulder with hers. "Well, one of us is. The other is a terrible something else."

"And you're the best," I added to soften our teasing. "We're lucky you put up with us."

Nadine straightened the bottom of her blossoming blouse. "Damn skippy." And on that note, she grabbed a sweet potato fry, dragged it through the ranch dressing, and happily gobbled it down.

I DROVE STRAIGHT FROM DINER TO THE NEW SHELTER THAT we'd built outside of town on ten beautiful acres. Parker and I had decided this morning we would ride to the sheriff's station together to give our statements, and I was running late. There were three vehicles parked outside the rescue. Parker's dually, Theresa's new minivan, and a small green hatchback I didn't recognize. We had four large fenced-in areas for the dogs to run and play. Keith, Theresa's boyfriend and soon-to-be-father of her baby girl, had Mike—a rambunctious white and black American Staffordshire terrier—outside in the right front area. Mike got the zoomies when he saw me, kicking up wet mud with every step, and I laughed. "Look at that boy go!"

"You're giving him his bath," Keith said with a smile. Mike, unlike a lot of pit bulls, didn't like showers or baths. Don't get me wrong, he loved getting dirty. Show him a puddle, a lake, or even just a bowl of mud, and Mike was all for it. But getting him clean was the bane of his existence.

I waved him off. "Not today." I walked down the path to the shelter's entrance. We used a keyless locking system to keep people from wandering in uninvited. The only visitors, other than the volunteers, were by appointment only. I punched in the code, and the light on the panel turned green. I turned the handle and opened the door a crack before the light could turn red again.

"Hey," I said to Keith. "Who's driving the hatchback?"

He shrugged. "Some blonde woman. She got here about twenty minutes ago. Parker let her in."

"Curly hair?"

Keith nodded. "Yeah. You know her?"

"Pretty sure I do." I took a deep breath and emotionally prepared myself as I entered the building. The scent of lemons and bleach was always the first thing I noticed when I came to the rescue. All of us who worked and volunteered here were careful to keep the place immaculately clean for the dogs in our care. The central heating kept the entire building a comfortable seventy degrees. Still, I braced myself for whatever chilly reception waited for me inside the office.

Theresa, close to full term now, sat in a wide swivel chair behind her desk. Mia Larson, Darren's wife, was sitting in a guest chair that she'd pulled up close to Theresa. She clutched a handful of tissue. Her eyes were puffy and her nose red, and when I strode inside the office, she jerked her gaze at me.

"Oh, Lily," she gasped as she rose to her feet. She crossed the room and hugged me. "I borrowed a coworker's car to come into Moonrise today to see you. I can't believe Rowdy's gone."

"I'm so sorry," I said as the knot from earlier reformed in my throat. "I'm so sorry for your loss." I glanced over at Theresa. She had tears in her eyes. She dabbed them away with the back of her hand.

"What am I going to do? I've lost my baby brother, and I can't lose my husband, too," she said fiercely. "Darren wouldn't have hurt Rowdy. Not for Rowdy's sake, you know, but for mine. I know my brother wasn't perfect, but I loved him. And Darren loves me."

"I understand," I said. "All too well."

She leaned back and looked me in the eye.

"My brother was killed a few years ago," I explained.

"Then you are the only one who could know," Mia said. "Will you help me?"

"If I can," I said, not sure if she meant funeral arrangements or calling extended family or friends. "What do you need?"

"I need you to find out who killed my brother, so he can get justice, and Darren can come home."

The matter-of-fact way that she stated her request startled me. "Why do you think—"

She peeped over her shoulder at Theresa. My very pregnant friend blanched.

"I've heard the stories of how you solved several murders in Moonrise. And not just from Theresa," she added, letting Theresa off the hook. "Will you help me, Lily? Will you find who did this to my brother, so he can rest in peace, and help me bring my husband home?"

CHAPTER 11

Unease rolled through me as Parker and I were escorted through the sheriff's station. In a room filled with gray cubicles, we were seated on a bench along the wall. I had several not-so-fond memories of this place, the least of which was being attacked by the previous sheriff in his office. I knew that a handful of the deputies blamed me for Sheriff Avery losing his job. But frankly, Avery had been lucky he hadn't served a nice long jail sentence. He would have deserved every day of it. Lucky for him, his wife Anna had turned state's evidence against a bigger fish. She had brokered a sweetheart deal for her and her husband, which kept them both out of jail.

I was glad for Theresa's sake that she didn't have to visit her folks in prison, but on the other hand, Avery had tried to kill me.

So, my feelings were understandably mixed.

Theresa and I had found our friendship again, and for that, I was glad. I'm not sure it would've been possible if I had pursued the assault charges. I had to content myself with the fact that they'd sold their home and moved away from Moonrise. Out of sight, out of mind.

Parker laced his fingers with mine. "I'll be glad to get this over. How long do you think they're going to make us wait?"

I was so caught up on my own past trauma related to this place, I hadn't noticed Parker's pinched expression or the closed-set of his shoulders. I gave his hand a squeeze. "Hopefully, not too long."

Gary Hall exited a door on the far side of the room. He cast me a scathing look as he crossed in front of us before disappearing behind one of the cubicles.

I tuned out the extraneous noises in the room, the blowers in the vents, the clicking of computer keys, and the low murmur of voices as I focused all my attention on Gary. I picked up on his and Deb Morton's voices but couldn't quite make out the words. I closed my eyes to hide the glowing green of my cougar rising to the surface and focused even harder.

"I don't buy it," I heard Hall say. "Those two are involved."

Morton sounded tired. "I don't see them shoving money down a guy's throat."

"I don't think Larson did this on his own," Hall countered.

"I'm not sure any of them did it." Morton's voice was strained now. "Let's just get this over with."

Morton stood up from a cubicle, walked to us, her face pale. Her hair was honey blonde and long enough that the end of her ponytail dangled between her shoulder blades. I'd seen her a few times now, and I still didn't have a good sense of her. Not yet.

She gestured between Parker and me. "Who wants to go first?"

"Parker," I said.

He gave me a startled look, but seeing my expression, he simply shrugged. "I guess I'll go first."

I wanted to hear exactly what he told Morton and Hall, in case they were planning to try and connect us to the case as more than witnesses. Gary Hall seemed to have a real bug up his butt about Parker and me, and I couldn't tell if it was reactionary or if he was a jerk.

Unfortunately, I miscalculated because Gary said, "Come with me, Ms. Mason. I'll take your statement."

I bit back a curse as I stood. I knew Parker's story wouldn't differ from mine, at least not to any significant degree, but the way Gary talked made me wonder if they planned to treat us like suspects instead of witnesses. I knew the routine by now, but still, I was unhappy when Morton took Parker into an interview room several doors down from the one Hall escorted me into.

"Have a seat, Ms. Mason." He gestured to the chair on the other side of a table.

I sat down. Deputy Hall did not. It was a psychological tactic to unsettle and intimidate me. Hall was wasting his time. I had been unsettled since I'd walked into the building.

He held a micro-recorder up for me to see. "Do you mind if I record your statement?"

"Go ahead."

"Deputy Gary Hall. Interviewing witness, Lily Mason," he said, then added the date and time. After, he set the recorder down on the table in front of me. He crossed his arms over his chest. "Why did you go to 405 Valley Road in Blaston at ten o'clock last night?"

"To check on our friend, Darren Larson."

"Why?"

"His wife called us. She was worried because he hadn't come home."

"What was he doing at that abandoned property?"

"Ask him."

"I feel like you're not cooperating, Ms. Mason. You need to tell me what you know."

I shrugged. "Mia Larson, the wife of Darren Larson, called me worried her husband hadn't returned from picking up supplies in town for their dog rescue. Parker had a message from Darren saying there was something wrong with the cameras at the abandoned house, so he was going over to check them out." I paused. "We'd rescued two abused pit bulls from the property the day before. He wanted to catch the abusers. That's what I know."

"So, then, you and Mr. Knowles decided to drive over there at ten o'clock at night?"

"Yes."

"When did you arrive?"

"About ten–thirty."

"It's a fifteen-minute drive from your place to Blaston."

"So?"

"What happened to the other fifteen minutes?"

"We had to get dressed and get the dogs into the car."

"Took you that long, huh?"

"Yes."

"What happened when you got to the property?"

"We found Darren on the basement staircase."

"What exactly did Mr. Larson say to you?"

"Rowdy's dead."

"And you decided to go see for yourself?"

Had I told Bobby that I checked Rowdy? I couldn't remember. I must have, though, since Deputy Hall was asking. Goddess, how did I always end up in the thick of it? "I have some medical training," I told the deputy. "I went to see if there was anything I could do."

"For a dead guy?" He paused. "You sure you didn't go into the basement for another reason?"

I kept silent. I refused to answer leading questions. Instead, I studied Hall. He was of average height and build, brown hair, and looked to be in his mid to late twenties. If it hadn't been for the gold rings that rimmed his blue eyes, I'd say his appearance was unremarkable.

He shifted uncomfortably under my gaze. Finally, he uncrossed his arms and sat down on the other side of the table. "What did you find when you went into the basement?"

"Rowdy was on the floor. On his back." I tried to be precise. "There was an overturned tub of kitty litter under the basement window. I checked Rowdy for a pulse—first, on his wrist and then on his neck. I couldn't find one. I saw a knife in the spilled litter. Then I heard shouting upstairs, and that's when I went up and saw you and your partner restraining Parker and Darren."

He squinted at me. "What did you see in the litter?"

"Black-handled survival knife. It looked chunky and heavy-duty. And don't worry, I didn't touch it."

Gary's breathing quickened. There was something wrong, but I didn't know what. "Is there anything else you want to add to your statement?"

"Only that after Parker and Darren were restrained, I went outside. My dogs were understandably scared, and when I went to check on them, you drew your weapon on me."

He flushed. "I thought you were running away."

I tried to keep the edge of anger out of my voice. And I admit, I let out some of my truth mojo. "And you were going to stop me by shooting me."

"A lot was going on at the scene, Ms. Mason. Your friend was yanking against the cuffs, we'd just found out there was a body in the basement, and you were running toward your truck. I just...reacted." He blinked at me, confused by his own confession. "But I don't have to explain myself to you."

But obviously, he'd wanted to. Otherwise, he wouldn't have. Bobby had told me about Hall's bad call that landed a child in the hospital. I supposed doing a job where half the people you dealt with were criminals or potential criminals could make you start painting everyone you met with the same suspicious brush.

I nodded to the door. "Can I go now? I don't have anything else to say."

"Someone will contact you if we have any follow up questions or if you are required to testify in court."

I got up from the seat. The metal chair legs made a

grating sound as they slid across the tiled floor. Hall's shoulders jerked up, and he forced them to relax.

"How long have you been on the job, Deputy Hall?"

"One year," he said. "But this place is just a stepping-stone to the FBI academy."

The young deputy had goals. If he didn't figure out how to manage his reactions, they were going to be thwarted before he even got started. "I hope it works out for you," I said.

"Thanks." He opened the door and ushered me out of the interview room. I looked around for Parker. I didn't find him, but I did see someone familiar. Rowdy's girlfriend sat on the bench where Parker and I had waited earlier. She wore tight jeans, pink cowboy boots, and a pink cashmere turtleneck sweater. Her legs were crossed, and her toe was bouncing.

I approached her. "Hello," I greeted. She glanced up at me without any recognition.

"Hi," she said with a clipped edge. "Do you know how long I'm going to have to wait? I have a manicure at two."

"I don't work here. I'm Lily Mason. We met yesterday in Blaston."

She scanned me up and down. "Did we?"

"I'm really sorry about your loss," I told her. She didn't look like a grieving girlfriend. "Can I ask you something?"

She smiled, then shook her head before waving pretty pink nails in my direction. "Go ahead. Ask."

"You and Rowdy looked awfully cozy yesterday, but you don't seem all that broke up that he's dead. How come?"

"Rowdy could be charming when he wanted to be, and

he was surprisingly good in the sack. However, for the most part, he was an entire son-of-a-bitch. And if he hadn't dumped me at Dally's bar last night and left me stranded in Moonrise, I might give two-nickels that he got himself killed. The way he did business, it was only a matter of time before someone got mad and tried to gut him."

I wasn't sure if his wound was public knowledge, so I asked. "How did you know someone sliced his stomach with a knife?"

"Racine." The sound of Deb Morton saying her name snapped her attention away from me. There was a look that passed between the two of them that I couldn't quite interpret.

I let it go. Parker looked as tired as I felt, and all I wanted to do was get him home.

Racine got up from the bench. "I've got a little advice for you, sweetie. Don't get yourself too worked up over the likes of Rowdy Dawson."

"I'll take that under advisement."

She stared at Parker. "Well, hello, handsome."

Parker draped his arm over my shoulders. "You ready to go?"

I flashed Racine a neener-neener glance—at least I hoped the neener was conveyed on some level—then said, "Good luck."

She scoffed. "I make my own luck." To Parker, she said, "If you ever get bored," she looked at me to make sure her point was made, "I work Mondays, Wednesdays, and most weekends at The Statesmen's Club out on Highway 20."

When we exited the station, I asked Parker, "What's The Statesmen's Club?"

"It's a juice bar," he said, as he took out his keys.

"So, it's a gym?"

Parker laughed. "No. Not a gym. A juice bar is a type of strip club. As long as they don't serve alcohol, the dancers can be fully nude."

Oh my gosh, Rowdy's girlfriend had been a stripper. Nadine's joke about the dollar bills seemed a little less funny now. I raised a brow at Parker. "You sure seem to know a lot about these juice bars."

He chuckled now. "You're the only woman I want to see fully naked."

"That's the right answer," I said, grinning.

CHAPTER 12

Late the next morning, I drove to The Cat's Meow. I wanted to talk to Buzz before the lunch crowd arrived. There was something wrong with him, other than his face being hair-challenged, and I was determined to get to the truth.

The breakfast rush was over, and he was standing at his grill, scraping the surface clean. The glorious aroma of bacon, sausage, and maple syrup still clung to the air. Dang it, I should have gotten here earlier. I knew Buzz would make me breakfast if I asked, but technically it would have been second breakfast since I'd eaten a large bowl of oatmeal and four pieces of heavily buttered toast a few hours earlier.

Buzz glanced up and smiled when he saw me. "Come on back."

I looked around. The place was empty except for a couple of elderly men drinking coffee in one of the booths.

"No Leon today?" I asked.

"He was here for the first two hours of the day, but he has classes, so he was stretching himself to help me out. Freda should be coming in soon for the lunch shift."

"Did you do breakfast by yourself?"

"Ah," he said with dismissal. "It wasn't that busy."

I joined him in the kitchen and took in the sink full of dirty dishes. "Not that busy, huh?"

He shrugged and tossed me a hand towel. "I was savin' them for you."

"Haha. You need to hire someone full-time to make up for the times when your part-time help can't work. And you had no idea I was coming in."

"I figured you'd get around to it eventually."

I turned on the hot water to fill the rinse sink. I'd helped out Buzz a few times before, so I knew the routine. Three sinks. Soapy water, rinse water, sanitizer. And the water had to be hot.

Buzz dumped the grease catch he removed from the front of the grill. "Go ahead and say what you've come to say, Lils."

Goddess, with that face and exasperated tone, I was having serious flashbacks to some of the conversations I'd had with Danny. I scraped plates as I spoke quietly to avoid being overheard by the old-timers. "Please tell me you've been shifting."

"I managed it a few times after we got back from California," he said. "But it's been getting more difficult. I haven't been able to turn at all in the past two months. Apparently, once you turn that switch off, it's harder to flip back on again."

I set down the dish in my hand and swiveled my gaze to him. "But you've been going to Johnson Shut-ins every month. What have you been doing on the full moon?" Unlike me, once Buzz had decided to integrate into a human town, he'd made it a practice of only turning cougar on the full moons when the tug of our second nature was the strongest.

I never went more than a few days without turning. It's the reason I bought property covered mostly in trees. It allowed me to be my two-natured authentic self.

Buzz grabbed a clean towel from a pile and dotted sweat bead from his forehead. "I've called the fertility doctor, and he said it should come back in time, as long as I keep trying."

"And what happens if it doesn't?"

Buzz sighed. "He said my years might catch up to my human side."

My mouth gaped.

"Yep," he said. "I'm seventy-six. If I don't start shifting soon, I'm going to start looking my age."

"You mean Pearl and Opal's age." I stared at him. "You know, if you had met Opal or Pearl when you were younger, they would have been young enough to date you."

Buzz snorted a laugh. "Pearl, maybe. I'm pretty sure I'm not Opal's type. Both women probably would have been the end of me."

"Probably," I giggled, then quickly sobered. "You need to talk to Nadine."

He shook his head. "She'll blame herself, and it's not her fault."

"Ridiculous. Nadine is your partner, Buzz. She has a right to know what's going on with you. Instead, you've left her to worry about all the worst-case scenarios."

Buzz arched his brow at me. "I think aging before her eyes, rapidly, over a short period of time, falls into that category."

"She's worried, Buzz. Her pregnancy is high risk. Stress is not good for her."

"Knowing isn't going to ease the worry," he said. "Not in this case."

"Sometimes knowing what the problem is, even if it's awful, can help you face it." I put my hand on his shoulder. "Tell her. You shouldn't be going through this alone."

"If I can't fix this, I'm going to end up alone, so I should get used to it."

I saw it now. This wasn't about getting some gray hair and wrinkles. Not entirely. Buzz was scared to lose Nadine. "She is more in love with you than some of the bonded shifters I know back home. It's a pure love that's not going to go away just because you get a little creaky in the joints."

"She will stay with me," he agreed. "But I'm not sure that's fair to her."

"Are you trying to make her leave?"

He shook his head. "I'm not that good of a man. I'll stick around as long as she puts up with me, but it'll hurt me every time I see the regret on her face."

I stared at him for a few seconds. "Wow. You put the Buzz in buzzkill."

His expression went from self-pity to surprise.

I didn't wait for him to formulate a response. "You are

the same man who put yourself through hell just to get the woman he loves pregnant, right? Because you kind of sound like a roasting weenie."

His tone grew almost menacing. "And how does a roasting weenie sound?"

"A little hissy and a lot of pissy."

"Is that so?"

The look of irritation totally took me back to all the times I'd lectured Danny. "Yep. So there."

We both crossed our arms and commenced a staring contest, with neither of us blinking for a full minute. Finally, Buzz tossed his towel into a basket next to his grill.

"I don't know what to do," he said.

"How about you don't keep things like this to yourself? You know I still have ties with Paradise Falls. My best friend's grandmother, who happens to be the grand inquisitor for witches, owes me a favor. I'll call it in and see if she can do anything to help."

Buzz frowned, then scratched his head and chuckled. "I'm being an idiot, aren't I?"

"You certainly are," I agreed.

"I'll talk to Nadine," he promised.

"Good." There was a special magic that happened when shifters turned together. It created a sort of electric sizzle in the air. It was one of the few, maybe the only thing, I missed about living in a supernatural community. However, maybe some of my magic could help Buzz. "The next full moon is Thursday. Come over, and we'll see if having another of your kind with you when you try to shift will facilitate the change."

Buzz nodded. "Thanks, Lily."

"You're welcome."

"Nadine tells me you've gotten yourself mixed up in another investigation."

I finished prepping the sinks and started placing plates and silverware into the soapy water to soak for a minute. "Are you really going to lecture me?"

"Nope," he said. "Just making conversation."

I handed him the towel and kissed his bare cheek. "You have a bunch of dishes to wash. Better get to it."

Ryan called me when I was on my way back to the shelter. "I found a tracking chip in Edward," he said.

My stomach sank.

"There's a possibility he might have been stolen," Ryan continued, telling me things I already knew. "I'm not obligated to call the owners, but I wanted to let you know. What would you like me to do?"

"Just hold off for now," I told him. "Does Elinor have a chip too?"

"No. Just him."

It didn't necessarily mean they came from different homes. Still, it was getting more and more likely, with only Elinor having been exposed to drugs and their byproducts, they'd hadn't been bonded long. It didn't mean their bond was any less intense, though. I planned to fight like crazy to keep them together. If Edward had come from a good home, maybe his family would want a second dog. It was wishful thinking on my part, but sometimes wishes came true.

"Do you have the owner's contact information?"

"Yes, why?"

"I'm going to check them out. If it looks like Edward came from a good home and he was stolen, we have to return him."

It would kill me to have to separate them, but if someone stole Smooshie, I would move heaven and earth to get her back. And Edward's family had taken the precaution of chipping him. That was a clear indication that they cared about him.

"Why don't you swing by at four? We'll check them out together."

"Okay," I said. "But only if I get to drive your car."

"Forget it. I'd ride shotgun in your little beat up S-10 before letting you behind the wheel of my baby."

"It's a deal. I'll pick you up at four." I hung up before he could backtrack. The idea of Ryan "Perfect Hair" Petry riding in my old, rusty Martha was a bright, shining light in an otherwise dismal day.

CHAPTER 13

"For heaven's sake, Lily, you need a new truck," Ryan complained. He lifted his legs a couple times to look under his thighs to see if he was getting his dress pants dirty or creased. "This eye-sore has seen better days."

"And it's seen me through some really bad ones," I told him. "This was the first thing in my life that I ever owned. The bank didn't own it. It wasn't a hand me down from my uppity neighbors. I worked two jobs, saving every last dime I could scratch together in order to pay for Martha."

His expression had changed from disgust to pity. "I'm sorry, Lily."

I clucked my tongue. "Don't go feeling sorry for me, now. I'm proud of every dent, crack, and speck of rust on this vehicle. As long as it will get me where I'm going, Martha isn't going anywhere."

"Fifteen years, huh? You started working at a young age."

"Yep." Dang it. Most folks in town thought I was in my early twenties, but I'd told my friends I was twenty-nine when I'd moved to town. Which would, in their eyes, make me around thirty now, not thirty-eight."

We'd been driving south of town for ten miles when I saw the liquor store outside of Blaston. Edward's owners had a rural address for somewhere outside of Centerville, the county seat of Remir. Ryan had GPS'd the address, so I relied on him to tell me when and where to turn.

Once again there were several vehicles, including the red Pontiac in the parking lot of the package store. It wasn't a hard leap to imagine, the way they tried to intimidate us off the property, that they were responsible for the pit bulls being tied up in the basement.

"What's going on?" Ryan asked. "You look like you're going to hulk out."

He wasn't far from the truth. "I'm feeling a bit edgy is all."

"I can imagine. You've had a traumatizing few days."

We drove through Blaston in the blink of an eye. A few miles later, there was a sign for Remir county. "That's close to Blaston," I said.

"Have you ever been to Centerville?"

I shook my head. "Up until this past week, I'd never been as far south as Blaston."

"Take a right up here on Highway 20."

"Oh, this is the road with the nudie bar," I said, remembering Racine's invitation to Parker.

"Are you taking a special interest in strip clubs?" Ryan asked. "I mean, if you need some extra hours..."

I hit his shoulder with the back of my hand. "How about you just give me a raise?"

"Evaluations are coming up," he teased. "We'll see what Abby has to say about you as an employee."

"Well, if that's the case, you better check your bank accounts, because I'm pretty sure Abby loves me, and she will want me to have a huge raise."

Ryan laughed. Then got quiet. "You know," he started, his tone serious. "If you're having money problems, you can always count on me. If I have it to give to you, it's yours."

"I'm okay, money-wise. I've been living on a little for years, so I don't spend outside my means. Hence, Martha," I told him. I put warmth into my smile. "But I appreciate knowing there's a Daddy Warbucks in town who has my back."

He laughed. "I do okay, but I'm no Warbucks. Honestly, Lily. You're one of the best people I know. I'd do just about anything for you."

"I feel the same about you." There was a sign on the highway that said, The Statesmen Club, and Live Nude Girls right under it. "That's real subtle," I said.

"I think that's what they're going for."

"Then result," I said. There weren't any cars parked out front except for two over-the-road semis. The sign on the door said open, and there was a tall privacy fence that stretched out the sides of the building and back. "Place looks a little dead. Why would they open on a Wednesday afternoon?"

"It's more crowded than you think," Ryan said. "You see that fence?"

I nodded. "That's blocking off a private parking lot. I think you'd be surprised at how many guys hang out at a place like this in the middle of a workday. The parking lot keeps their customers on the down low."

"And how do you know all this?"

His gaze lingered for a moment. "I was pretty darn good at playing straight for most my life. Including and not limited to going to the occasional strip joint." His breath fogged the glass window. He drew a smiley face then wiped it away. "I'm glad it warmed up a little."

"I'm not sure I am. At least when the ground was frozen, I wasn't sinking in mud holes. Since the thaw last night, the ground is basically mush." And I knew from last year and the year before that Missouri weather always found a way to compound misery. It would freeze, and the mud would turn to ice. Then it would melt, and we'd get mud again. Then it would freeze then melt then freeze, etc. Never giving the ground time to dry out in between. By the end of last winter, I'd ruined two pairs of cute winter boots from sinking ankle deep in the sludge. Uck.

"That's why you need to pave your drive," Ryan said.

"At this rate, I'll need to pave my whole yard," I countered. "Which is why a raise would come in handy."

He didn't rise to the bait this time. "Turn up here on 952 road."

The Edison's lived at 33 SE 952, which meant we were close. My gut began to churn. I hoped they were great. And if they were, I hoped they'd take Elinor as well. I put on my blinker and waited as a car came roaring around the corner just up ahead. I recognized the blue sports car right away. It was Racine. She saw me, and I don't know whether she recognized me or not. Either way, it didn't stop her from flipping me the bird as she passed by.

Ryan's expression was pure shock and outrage. I, on the other hand, laughed hard and loud. If Racine hadn't flirted so hard with my man, I'd probably like her.

"What in the world was that all about? You weren't even doing anything," Ryan complained.

"My feelings aren't hurt," I said. "That woman's got bigger problems than me."

"Like what?"

"Well, her ex-boyfriend died the night they broke up, and she works at that hole in the wall back there with all the private parking."

Ryan looked at me. "She does have a nice car. Maybe you should consider a change in career."

I patted the dash before turning on to the rural road. "There, there, Martha. Don't listen to him." I cast a sideways glance at Ryan. "If she breaks down on us out here, it's your fault."

"Not hardly."

The GPS took us nearly to the exact location. But the driveway for the address was about a hundred feet past the spot on the internet map. A white two-story farmhouse in need of some maintenance, but otherwise in decent shape, was nestled in a copse of trees. There was a pole barn off to the left, and a small single-wide trailer just beyond that. I'd seen similar setups back home when kids and such would move back to their parents' property. The trailer had winterizing plastic taped around the outside windows and there was a padlock on the door.

I heard the bark of dogs, and the whirring of a heat pump as I cut the engine and got out of the truck. Ryan joined me. "I'm not sure I like the look of this place."

I saw it differently. Sure, there were signs of poverty, but being poor didn't make you unworthy. The Edison's kept a tidy yard, their porch was salted, and they had enough gravel in the drive to keep a vehicle from sinking.

We'd decided early on to act like we were fund raising to give free vaccinations and spaying and neutering for loving families that had pets but couldn't afford medical checkups. These were things that Ryan would do for free and had many times. However, money for supplies was always welcome. Every dollar counted.

I made a face.

"Is something the matter?" Ryan asked.

"Twenty-two dollars," I said.

"For what?"

"Why would someone shove twenty-two one-dollar bills down someone's throat?"

"Is this a hypothetical?"

"Sure," I replied. I didn't know what the police were making public as far as Rowdy's death went, but I knew Ryan wouldn't spread information like that around. "Let's say a guy is murdered in an abandoned house. His stomach is slashed, and twenty-two one-dollar bills are wadded up and shoved down his throat. Why?"

"Okay, so not hypothetical. Jayzus, is that what happened to Rowdy Dawson?"

"Did you know him?" I asked.

"Of him," he said. "He went to Centerville High School with a...friend of mine from back then."

"Like Mark Stephens was your friend?" Ryan and Mark had hooked up in high school, but things hadn't ended well between them. Mark was so deep in the closet he would probably never come out.

"Maybe," Ryan said coyly. "It was just a little bit of fun. His name was Alex. He had the prettiest green eyes."

I laughed as we strolled to the door.

"Why are you laughing?" Ryan asked.

"His last name wasn't Naples, was it?"

He frowned. "How do you know that?"

I opened the screened door and knocked then let the screened door close. "It turns out you and Nadine had a lot in common in high school."

He grinned. "I'd forgotten she'd dated him."

I heard more barking inside the house and the voice of a man say, "Settle down, Matilda. Go on now."

"Someone's coming," I whispered.

"How do you know?" Ryan asked, matching my quiet. "And why are we whispering?"

An old man in coveralls with thick glasses, a balding dome and a thick snowy beard opened the door. "Can I help you folks?" He rubbed the bridge of his nose.

"Hello, sir," I started. "Are you Timothy Johnson?"

His gaze turned suspicious. "I'm Lester Johnson. Timothy is my youngest grandson. Why are you asking about him? Is that boy in trouble again? I can't bail him out anymore. If you're here to collect some debt, you'll have better chance of finding gold nuggets in an outhouse."

"No, sir, we're not here to collect any money," I said, going completely off script. "I am part owner in a pit bull rescue up and a veterinarian technologist in Moonrise, and, in partnership with Petry's Pet Clinic," I gestured to Ryan, "this is Doctor Petry, our local veterinarian. We are trying to bring awareness to the problem of abused and abandoned pets, while offering services to the community like free checkups for your pets. Do you have a pet you'd like us to check out?"

Ryan took out his wallet and handed the elderly man a card. "I'm at your service."

"Matilda has something growing from her eyelid," he said. "I wouldn't mind if you took a gander." He swung the door wide open then turned on his heel with the expectation we'd follow.

"Matilda better not be his wife," Ryan muttered out the side of his mouth.

I giggled and elbowed Ryan in the ribs. "Hush."

The living room had a potbelly stove with a pipe fitted to vent through the wall and outside, two old, but comfortably looking couches, a recliner, and a dozen crocheted afghans covering the backs and seats of all the furniture.

There were pictures on the television stand of Lester and a woman at various times in their lives. There was a black and white photo of a thin man, who kind of looked familiar, holding the woman in his arms, they were both smiling. Over the years, the photos took on a touch of severity. By the last picture on the shelf, their smiles in the photo didn't reach their eyes.

"Are these of you and your wife?" I asked when he

walked the biggest Bullmastiff I'd ever seen—and I'd seen several of the breed during my time in Moonrise—into the living room.

"Yep," Lester said. "That was my Lucy. She passed away two years ago." He shook his head. "Heart attack. Damn hospital sent her home, told us she had heart burn. I woke up the next morning." He sighed. "Lucy didn't."

I was constantly reading medical journals, and for more than a decade, heart doctors and researchers have been telling anyone who will listen that women are just as prone to heart attacks and heart disease as men, but our symptoms aren't always so obvious. And it's the leading cause of death in women, which just made it all the scarier. A simple blood test and an electrocardiogram could have saved Lucy's life.

However, bringing all that up to Lester now, would not raise his Lucy from the dead, so I blew out a breath and let it go.

Ryan was sitting on the edge of the couch now, trying to find light to look at Matilda's eyelid growth. Lester gave him an odd look. "Didn't you bring any equipment?"

Ryan eyeballed me. "Good question."

"This is just a courtesy visit to garner interest in the more rural areas. We'll come back with the right equipment next time." My answer wasn't great, but luckily, Lester seemed to accept it.

"I appreciate it mightily. Matilda is my only companion these days."

"Your grandson doesn't come around?"

"Hell no," Lester barked. He sat down in his easy chair and pushed it back to its reclined position. "That boy has always been no good. But Lucy loved him. She said he reminded her of me when we were young." The gentleman sneered. "Maybe in looks, but certainly not when it came to work. Always one scheme after another. If you ask me, he's the reason Lucy had her heart attack in the first place."

I couldn't shake that I recognized the man in the black and white photo. Did I know Lester's grandson? Had I seen him somewhere before? "Do you have any photos of Timothy?"

"Check that drawer over there," Lester said. "Lucy used to keep all kinds of them in there, and I've never bothered to clean it out."

"Does Timothy have a dog, too?" I asked as I opened the drawer and took out a stack of photographs.

"Yeah, a red nose pit bull named Tobacco. Dumb name for a dog, but he had the prettiest brown fur you ever did see. He was a sweetheart too. It's too bad Matilda is a one dog per house kind of dog, or I might have kept Tobacco went I sent that kid packing., I'd do it again. I found a stash of drugs out in my pole barn a few months after my Lucy died. That was it for me. I padlocked the door on the trailer so he couldn't come back."

"I don't blame you," I said. Drugs had been the ruin of my brother. I never kicked him out of the house, but there were a few times I wanted to do just like Lester had. Most of the pictures were baby pictures. Lester and his wife had two kids, a girl and a boy, it looked like. Eventually, I hit the jackpot. As I stared at the photo of the young man with dimples so deep it looked as if someone had cut his cheeks, I asked Lester absently, "Does your grandson go by the name of Larry?"

"Yes," he said. "His middle name is Lawrence, and he's always gone by Larry. It's why I thought you were here to collect money. No one who knows him calls him Timothy."

Well, wasn't that something else. "It's a small world," I murmured. Timothy was none other than Larry Johnson aka red Pontiac guy aka the guy who was never getting his dog back.

CHAPTER 14

Nadine was the first person I contacted after leaving Lester Johnson's farmhouse. Ryan and I went to his clinic and picked up the red phosphorous rag to deliver it to the sheriff's department. Ryan had placed it in a sealed specimen bag, but since I hadn't followed any chain of custody when I'd retrieved it, I was doubtful it could be used as evidence. Still, it was better to err on the side of too much information rather than not enough.

However, I let Ryan do the delivering. I wanted to go back to the station house like I wanted a third nostril. Not at all. Instead, I headed home to my warm house with my warm hunka-hunka to spend an evening alone with him and the fur kids. Right now, that sounded like heaven coated in ice cream and marshmallow fluff, breaded and deep-fried, all on a stick.

And now, I was hungry.

The lights were on when I got home. The front door opened, and Smooshie leaped from the porch and barreled at me. She jumped the last couple of feet, and I caught her midair as she took us both down.

I groaned as she happily licked my face. "You're a menace," I told her as the cold and wet seeped into my pants. I sat up as Parker laughed and laughed. A few times, he stopped breathing. I gave Smooshie a playful cuff on her ear. "Brat," I said. "It's a good thing I love you."

I got up and picked the larger chunks of mud and such off me as I approached Parker in the doorway. "How about a hug, honey?"

"Nope!" But he zigged when he should have zagged, and I wrapped my arms around his waist and sunk into his warm and comforting embrace.

I sighed. "This is so nice."

"Bad day?" he asked as he held me without any expectation of when it would end.

"I love that you hug me as long as I want."

"If given the chance, I'd never let you go," he replied. "We'd just be glued at the hips."

I breathed in his scent. Mint, juniper, and honey. Home. Love. Happiness. "That would make having sex difficult."

"You're right." He chuckled. "I didn't think that through very well."

"No, you didn't." Beyond Parker's scent, I detected the delicious aroma of Parker's spaghetti with meat sauce and garlic bread. It was the first meal he ever made me, and it had been my favorite ever since. "You made me dinner."

"That I did." He kissed the top of my head, but he didn't let me go. "I figured since you'd skipped lunch, you'd be starving tonight."

"I am so hungry. Even dog treats sound yummy."

Parker laughed. "That's gross."

I know he would hold me all night if I let him, but the bread started to smell charred, and I needed food in me sooner, not later. "Okay, I'm good," I told him.

He rubbed my back then let me go. "You get washed up and in some dry clothes. I'll set the table."

When I got out of the shower, I put on my oldest and most comfortable, almost paper-thin, jammy bottoms, and one of Parker's white tank undershirts. After the day I'd had, I was ready for pure relaxation. After dinner, of course.

The moment I walked out into the living room, I instantly regretted my choices.

"Hey, Babe. Darren and Mia have stopped by," Parker said.

Uninvited, I added mentally but didn't say it. The couple had experienced a much more difficult week than I had, so the least I could do is be kind. "Hi, you two. I'll be right back." I jogged to our bedroom, grabbed Parker's flannel robe, put it on, and rejoined them.

Smooshie was sniffing Darren and Mia's legs as if they were an aroma puzzle that only she could solve.

I snapped my fingers, amazed when she actually came over to me and sat down at my feet.

Darren's eyes were dark-rimmed and exhausted. The two nights in the county jail had really done a number on him.

"It's good to see you both," I said. "I'm glad Darren is out of jail."

Mia shook her head. "The judge granted bail today. It's

taken me this long to get it posted, so I could take him home." She looked at me. "We won't stay long, but is it okay if Bear comes in? He's out in the truck waiting on us, but I think he really needs to be with Darren right now."

"Absolutely," I said. "Should I put Smooshie in our room?"

"Bear does well with other dogs. They should be fine together." She went outside.

"Have a seat, Darren. Can I get you something to drink?"

"I'll take a beer if you have it."

I looked at Parker. "I've got some microbrew in the garage fridge."

Darren smiled, and it eased the tension in his face. "I'm not a fan of artisanal alcohol, but beggars, and in this case, me, will not be choosers."

"Be right back," Parker said.

And then it was just the two of us. "Darren, can I ask you something?"

"Would it do it any good if I said no?"

"Yes. If you don't want to give me any information, I won't pry. But I'm a good investigator, and if you let me help you, I'll do everything in my power to prove your innocence."

He pivoted his eyes to me. "Mia said you're a go-getter."

I shrugged. "Takes one to know one, I suppose."

"She says she recognizes a fellow survivor when she sees one." He shook his head and rubbed his bald dome. "Do you think people get what they deserve?"

I didn't understand why he was asking the question. Did he feel he deserved something? Some kind of punishment?

Or a reward? I wasn't sure he was going to like my answer either way. "I don't believe in karma if that's what you mean. Good things happen to bad people. Bad things happen to good people. There is no rhyme or reason to it, and I don't sit around waiting for some mystical energy to decide my fate. When bad things happen, I work the problem, find a solution, and put a plan in action to fix it. It's not usually quick, sometimes it's messy, but in the end, I get there.

"And when good things happen?" he asked.

I smiled. "It took me a long time to trust good things," I told him. "I think you know what I mean when I say that. Good things lead to hope, and hope, when thwarted, is a soul killer. Or I used to think that way."

"And now?"

"Now, when good things happen, I freaking celebrate. You have to take the joy when it comes and commit it to memory so that if the bad times come back, you have something to hold onto." I remembered the first time Parker kissed me. I savored the moment, replayed it several times, then played it again.

"Damn," Darren said. "That must have been a good one. Your smile is practically blinding me."

"That's joy, my friend."

He chuckled, and his tension eased even more. "I'll give joy a try," he said.

"Who's Joy? And why are you giving her a chance?" Mia asked as she came back inside. It turned out that Bear was a red and black bloodhound who stood as tall as Elvis and had the loosest, most gorgeous floppy jowls.

"He's beautiful," I said. I didn't pet him, no matter how much I wanted to, and my fingers were definitely itching to get some pets in on that hound. Bear was a service dog, and right now, Darren needed him, which meant it would be rude and selfish to distract Bear from his purpose.

"We love him so much," Mia said.

I grabbed Smooshie by the collar before she could get in her usual nose-in-the-butt greeting. Bear went right to Darren, sat down between his knees, and put his ginormous head onto Darren's thigh. "Such a good boy." I glanced down at Smooshie, who was leaning against my leg now. "You're a good girl," I told her. "In your own special way." The kind of special that meant total, loveable derp.

"Go ahead and ask your questions, Lily," Darren said. "I think I do want your help."

Mia's eyes brimmed with tears. When I looked at her, she shook her head. She didn't want to draw attention to whatever emotions she was experiencing.

Instead, I asked Darren, "What did you see on the camera? The reason you called Parker that night."

He combed his beard with his fingers. "It was strange. I got an alert that the front driveway camera had been activated. I checked out the footage, and there was a short clip of Rowdy's SUV pulling up to the house. I didn't think much of the fact that he'd gotten out of the vehicle on the passenger side. I figured he'd had a few, and a friend had driven him."

"Not girlfriend," I said.

"It didn't look like Racine. The driver wore a bulky coat with the hood up, so it was difficult to tell who it was. Same when the cameras were triggered in the house. I was pissed off until I saw the basement footage. He was on the ground, and the guy in the coat was holding something in his hand." He looked up at his wife and choked up. "I'm sorry, Mia. So sorry."

She went and sat next to him and put her hand on his back. "You don't get to make yourself responsible for Rowdy. Don't do that, okay. You didn't kill him." The tears in her eyes fell onto her cheeks. I could see now that Mia was a tower of strength for Darren. She and I had very different personalities, but some of our experiences had shaped the way we dealt with trauma. Some people shut down in a crisis, but it was a place where we both could shine. "I want some justice for Rowdy, no matter what kind of choices he'd made. He was still my brother, and I will do what I can to fight for him. I always have. So, go ahead and tell Lily the rest."

He nodded, but I could see his reluctance. "I was fifteen minutes away at the store when it happened. I thought I saw something else. I didn't know I was watching him die." He groaned. "Another car showed up, and I swear I thought he might be having a party. It had made me angry. He knew I'd put up cameras to catch the guys who'd tied up those dogs."

I thought about how worried his wife had been when he hadn't come home. "How come you didn't call Mia?"

He took her hand and held it tight. "I didn't call her because I didn't want her to worry about Rowdy. He's already put her through so much." He let go of her and ran his hands over Bear's head and neck now. "I took my time driving over. I might have saved Rowdy if I hadn't. But by the time I found him, he'd already bled out."

My brow lowered. "The police didn't tell you?"

"Tell him what?" Mia asked.

"Rowdy's wound didn't kill him."

She sat forward on the couch. "Then what did?"

"He was choked to death."

Mia paled then shook her head. "Dear Lord, Rowdy. What in the world had you gotten yourself into?"

CHAPTER 15

On Thursday, I woke up feeling the moon all the way to my bones. I thought about Buzz as I drove into town to meet Nadine and Reggie for coffee. The three of us all had busy lives, but Thursday morning coffee, and at least two lunches a week, enabled us to catch up with all the personal things going on in our lives and keep us close.

It was Reggie's turn to host coffee at her house, and I couldn't have been more excited. She had one of those super fancy espresso—will curl your hair, shave your legs, and walk your dog—machines. Nadine was already there sipping on a decaf vanilla latte with fresh whipped cream, extra sugar, extra vanilla when I arrived. Reggie had whipped me up a caramel macchiato double whip, sprinkled with sea salt and drizzled with chocolate sauce.

I sat down at Reggie's kitchen breakfast bar and cupped my cold hands around the warm mug. "You know, if you ever get tired of doctoring, you can always fall back on barista work."

Reggie was a purest when it came to Espresso, and she was drinking a double shot in a tiny demitasse cup. She had her straight, black hair down around her shoulders, a rare sight. As a surgeon and medical examiner, Reggie tended to keep her hair back and up in a tight bun. As a doctor, she appeared practical and professional. But with her hair down, she reminded me of an Italian Vogue cover model. Thin, tall, pale skin, brown eyes, narrow face, and an aquiline nose framed out by silky black hair.

"If I ever get tired of doctoring," she replied. "I'll keep that in mind."

"Speaking of doctoring, have you found out anything more from the autopsy?" I asked.

"I should have the tox screens back today, along with other labs."

"Can you get fingerprints off the money you pulled from his throat?" Nadine asked.

"Liz Harris is working on it. She says that there are at least fifty different partials on every bill. It's going to be difficult to match someone not in the system."

"If Darren's print isn't among the multitude, does that help clear him?" I asked. "He and Mia stopped by last night, and I don't think he'll survive prison. He's pretty fragile."

"There's something you should know, Lily. Darren and Rowdy got into a huge fight that afternoon at the Mini-mart in Centerville," Nadine said. "The security cameras got him shoving Rowdy against the building. He shouted something to the effect of, Mia would have been better off letting you rot in foster care."

Why hadn't Darren told me about the fight? Was he

trying to protect Mia? Or himself? I'd seen the way the woman looked at Darren. I didn't think an argument with Rowdy would have changed the way she felt about her husband. "Did Darren say what the argument was about?"

"He said he'd heard some rumors about Rowdy and the guys running drugs in Blaston. He said he suspected that Rowdy knew more about how the dogs ended up in that basement."

"And did Rowdy confess to him?"

Nadine shook her head. "No. Rowdy called him a coward and said something about Mia deserving to be with a real man. Someone who wasn't damaged."

"That's not motive, though. Families fight." I knew from personal experience.

"It's another piece of the puzzle," she said. "They fought. Harsh words were exchanged, and it got violent. Add in Darren's admission that he was angry when he drove to Blaston that night, and he was covered in Rowdy's blood when the deputies arrived. It makes for an excellent circumstantial case. The only thing missing is the smoking gun. Or, in this case, the bloody knife."

"Wait? What?"

"You know what I mean. The weapon wasn't recovered at the scene."

"I know what you mean," I told her. "But I saw the knife. The weapon was there, a black-handled military-style utility knife. It was lying in the spilled litter. I find it hard to believe that the crime techs missed it."

Reggie's brow furrowed. "Harris and O'Rourke are

meticulously thorough. If there had been a knife in that basement, they would have found it."

I met Nadine's look of consternation with my own. "I saw what I saw. It was there. I swear it."

"If you say you did, then I believe you," Nadine said. "I'll ask Gary and Deb if anyone else went into the basement."

"And I'll talk to the crime techs and see if they thought any part of the scene looked as if someone had tampered with it," Reggie added. She turned the beautiful circle-cut diamond set in a gold band on her left ring finger with her thumb. Something she did when she was worried.

To ease the tension, I asked, "Have you guys set a date yet?"

She nodded as she let out a slow breath. "We're thinking this coming summer when CeCe is home from college." She stared out the French doors off her modern kitchen and out into the backyard. She'd landscaped it the first year she and CeCe had moved to Moonrise, and it had a large patio, a gazebo, and a fountain that had been drained and covered for the winter. Her property was in a ritzier neighborhood, and she had most of her three acres surrounded by a privacy fence. "We might do it here. Keep it small, you know. Just close family and a few friends."

"You better be counting us in the family column," Nadine said.

"Absolutely," Reggie acknowledged. "Right up there with the creepy uncle whose all hands and the aunt with the mustache who always has her mouth open when she goes in for a kiss," she teased.

I guffawed. "Who are you related to? And how can I avoid them."

"Don't worry. Uncle Rogerio and Auntie Carlotta are not invited." She waved a hand. "They've been put on a no-fly list since Auntie Carlotta tried to sneak a bird onto a plane after a visit to New York City a few years back."

"A bird? Was it a pet? They probably could have gotten permission to take the bird on board if they would have asked the airline."

Reggie grimaced and sat on a stool on the opposite side of the counter. "It was a pigeon. And not one that belonged to them."

Nadine barked a laugh. "Hah! They stole a pigeon. Who does that?"

"It was a homing pigeon, too, not just one of the many millions of pigeons crapping all over New York. No. They had to take one that was an elite champion pigeon who had been tagged with a tracker. Even worse, the pigeon got loose on the plane. That was a poop-show of epic proportions. Literally. They say it's lucky when a bird craps on you, but I think there were about a hundred people on that flight who would beg to differ."

I laughed at the incredulity. "How in the world did your aunt and uncle get a live pigeon past security."

"Apparently, it was easy. My aunt had put the pigeon in a small box. She poked a couple of holes in the top of the box and stuck it in her purse. It went through the x-ray as still as could be, and the security officer who saw it thought it was a souvenir. Auntie Carlotta was never searched. And when she got on the plane, she waited until the jet was taxiing down the runway to open the box to give the bird fresh air. Big mistake. The pilot had to turn the plane around and dock again. The airport called the police. They escorted my aunt and uncle off the plane and out of the terminals.

"Did they go to jail?" Nadine asked.

"They were in their late seventies, so the judge let them off with time served. But the airlines...they never forget. Hence, the no-fly list."

I grinned. "So...it was a case of no harm...no fowl." I laughed at my own joke. "Get it. Fowl, like birds. Not foul, like baseball."

Nadine shook her head and groaned.

But Reggie laughed. "I get it. And I will probably use it the next time I tell the story." She smiled. "The good news is, they can't fly to Missouri and ruin my wedding."

"Who can't ruin the wedding?" Greer Knowles asked as he walked into the kitchen. Greer was a fit man in his fifties, handsome, graying hair, and light blue eyes that he'd passed down to my beau, Parker. I knew, without a shadow of a doubt, that if Parker aged like his dad, I was a lucky girl.

"Creepy aunt and uncle," Reggie replied.

"Ah, the bird thieves." He kissed Reggie. "Morning, beautiful."

Her face flushed with pleasure. "Morning."

He grabbed a biscotti from a cookie jar on the counter. "How come you all are here so early?"

I raised a brow at him. "I could ask you the same. Don't you have a shop to open?"

"I shut down for two weeks of vacation." He frowned.

"You know, this is the first time I've ever taken that much time off of work."

"You'll need it to finish moving in," said Reggie.

"I guess that answers the question about where the newlyweds will live," said Nadine, grinning.

I was happy for Reggie and Greer, but I had to take a moment to process the information and what it would mean for Parker. "What are you doing with your house, Greer?"

"I don't know yet," he said. "I want to talk to Parker first. But I can't live in the past anymore. It's time to move on."

Parker had grown up in that home. It was a place filled with memories of his mother, rest her soul, and I'd seen him wrestle a few times with the idea that Greer was moving on with his life. Even so, Parker was happy for his dad. Above all people, he knew that when you got a chance for real happiness, you took it.

"He'll be glad you're getting on with your life," I told Greer.

"I hope so," he said.

I gave Greer a hug then did the same with Reggie. "I'm thrilled for you guys. And a summer wedding in the backyard sounds perfect."

I walked to the door and visualized the yard full of chairs, a few tents for food and presents. There was definitely enough room for a small, gorgeous affair. The back deck was partially covered and would be perfect for an open bar. I noticed a yellow tub full of colorful items under the table. "Do you have toys in that tub out there?"

"For Smooshie and Elvis," Greer clarified. "Sometimes I

bring them over here when I have them. The yard is big enough for them to have room to play."

Reggie grinned. "I do love it when they come over. Elvis likes to hang out with me in the kitchen, while Smooshie gives Greer a workout."

"I thought giving Greer a workout was your job," Nadine muttered just loud enough for everyone to hear.

I giggled. "You're certainly on a roll today."

"Buzz has been in a better mood this week," she said. "From what I hear, thanks to you. I'm glad you talked to him."

She didn't bring up the fact that he wasn't shifting, so I avoided mentioning it. "He's coming out to the house tonight. It's a full moon, so we're going to run together."

"Dang, girl." Greer cleared his throat. "I forget most of the time that you occasionally change into a giant cat."

"Meow." I mimed a claw swipe at him.

He grinned as he grabbed a coffee from a regular eight-cup coffee maker. "On that note, I have boxes to move. Give my grandpuppies a pet for me and tell Parker I'll come by the rescue tomorrow. We can talk about the house then."

Reggie's house was massive. Four bedrooms with an open floor plan. And Greer was right. The backyard was perfect for a couple of big dogs. Which gave me an idea. "I think your love story might deserve another," I said. Then I proceeded to tell them all about the bonded pair of pit bulls named Edward and Elinor.

CHAPTER 16

Chapter Sixteen
The evening temperatures dropped down to twenty-seven degrees, cold enough to harden the ground. The clouds parted and basked in the glorious beams of light bouncing off the full moon.

Buzz and I drove Martha to the edge of the woods back behind the house while Nadine and Parker sat down to a sporting game of Gin-Rummy, wagering a penny a point. My BFF was a shark when it came to cards. The last time they played Parker owed her thirty-six dollars. That's a lot of freaking pennies.

Buzz and I sat on the open tailgate of my truck, preparing to let our fur out.

He tilted his head back to bask in the moonbeams. His stubble was already thick enough to create a mahogany shadow over his jaw and upper lip. He was growing the beard out like he'd promised Nadine, and I felt a pain at never seeing that face again. Moonlight caught his auburn hair and made it look as if the fire was dancing along the strands. My hair was more cinnamon in color, but there was no denying our family resemblance.

"Are you ready?" I asked him.

"Sure," he said. "Let's give it a try."

Nudity wasn't an issue in shifter societies. Still, Buzz and I had lived among humans long enough to feel strange about stripping down in front of each other. He took one side of the truck, and I went to the other.

I cheated by raising my fur to the surface of my skin before I disrobed. It made the chilly wind bearable.

"Damn, it's freezing out here," Buzz complained.

"It'll get warm quick enough once you get furry." I scratched my nose and sneezed as I caught the end of a whisker. Whiskers for all cats, even shifters, were highly sensitive. Our whiskers helped us to see and make sense of objects near us. They were also great for detecting subtle shifts in the movement of air near and around us. This came in handy when hunting. With the moon's fevered energy upon me, oh boy, was I ready to hunt. "Let's go."

Shifting was nothing like the movies. Fiction tended to depict the turning as a violent act against a shifter's human side, skin and muscle ripping, bones breaking and reforming, as the person transformed into a monster. On the contrary, shifting into my cougar form felt more like soaking in a hot tub after taking muscle relaxers and Xanax. It wrapped me like a warm embrace and made me feel like no matter what happened, it would all be okay. I swear, if modern medicine could bottle the feeling, it would be the catalyst that finally brought about world peace.

I stretched my front legs, my tail twitching back and forth, and I let the sense of well-being flow through me. I heard Smooshie barking from inside the house. Poor baby. She was feeling replaced. Tomorrow night I'd go running with her, and all would be forgiven.

I kicked my back feet out, testing the pads of my paws against the frozen ground. Not slick. I was about four times larger than a domestic cat in my cougar form, and I weighed ninety-eight pounds. I was also stronger and faster than your average one-natured cougar. I could run fifty-six miles per hour—I knew this because Nadine had insisted on using her speed gun to time me—and I could leap over thirty feet.

I prowled around the back of the truck and was surprised that Buzz was still in his birthday suit. I pulled my lips back, revealing my teeth as I rasped out a sound of annoyance.

Buzz shook his head and put his pants back on.

Well, crap. I scampered back to my pile and changed, cursing as the abrupt shift from warm confident cougar to scared and anxious human. It was like getting hit in the face with a bucket of ice.

"Buzz." I put my clothes on as quickly as I could. "What happened?"

He jumped on the tailgate and waited for me. "Nothing," he said flatly. "That's the problem."

"Can you feel the moon?" Maybe his second nature had been cut off from the magic.

He nodded. "I do. I feel like I'm a pressure cooker with a faulty valve. Too much steam and nowhere to vent it."

"Don't pressure cookers explode when that happens?"

He blew out a long slow breath and nodded.

I put my arm around his back. "I don't want you to explode. Maybe you're overthinking it. What's going on in your head when you get ready to change?"

"Oh, nothing much. Just thinking about a diner that won't run itself. Worrying that the woman I love with every bit of my soul will have to watch me age and die. And if I do start shifting again, then I'm going to have to watch her age and eventually die, and..." He scrubbed his face. "Damn it, why did I shave my damn beard?"

"Because of the woman you love with every bit of your soul."

He smiled sheepishly. "Right."

"What else are you worried about?"

He turned to me and met my gaze. His voice was barely audible, but I heard every word. "What if I outlive my kids?"

The weight of his question settled onto me. The heaviness of his anxiety was palpable. "Buzz, you're going to kill yourself worrying about outcomes that you have no control over."

"I want to shift, Lily. I really do."

I shook my head. "I don't think so." I'd call my friend Hazel tomorrow and see if her grandmother had been able to find a fix for Buzz, but until then, all I could do was show him my love and support. I gave him a peck on the cheek, already rough with the new growth. "Why don't we head up to the house? It's still early. The four of us could have dinner and relax."

"Thanks, Lils. I'd like that."

As we drove toward the house, I heard a familiar engine

roar as a vehicle turned off the main road and shot down my drive. I pushed the gas pedal down and sped up.

"You expecting company?" Buzz asked.

"Nope."

"Do you think it's friend or foe?"

I slid to a stop in our front yard. "I wish I knew." I put Martha in park and jumped out. The car, headlights on high beam, idled behind Parker's dually. I took a few steps toward it and recognized the voice of the man behind the wheel.

"Well," he said. "You must be Lily Mason, vet and pit bull rescuer."

"Son of a—" It was Red Pontiac Larry. I looked over my shoulder. Buzz was behind me, and Parker and Nadine had stepped out onto the porch. "Get them inside and call the police," I hissed to Buzz.

He didn't question me. His instinct to protect his mate took over. He jogged up to the house and rushed Nadine inside. Parker was off the porch and running toward me.

"Stop right there," Larry shouted. He cut his engine, and I could hear the slide of a shotgun being loaded.

"He's got guns," I said loud enough for Parker to hear.

Parker froze in place. He was army trained to assess a situation and act in the best interest of his team. In this case, his team was me. "What do you want?" Parker asked Larry. Parker was trying to move the target from me to himself.

Larry and two of his buddies got out of the car. Larry had his pistol in his hand and a cigarette dangling from his lips. I suspected he'd watched too many John Wayne movies. Only John Wayne was supposed to be the hero. His buddies carried shotguns, and I dubbed them Shotgun Bros #1 and #2.

Larry squared his shoulders at Parker. "I want your bitch to give me back my dogs." He lifted his gun. "And I want you to shut up."

Fear gripped me. "They're not here," I said, desperate to have him point his weapon anywhere else.

Smooshie was barking and growling inside the house, and I prayed to the goddess that no one let my girl outside. She was terrible with commands, and I wouldn't be able to stop her charging. I calculated in my head how fast I would have to be to get in front of a bullet's path if this dog-abusing monster shot at her.

"Keep Smooshie inside," I shouted. Larry and his friends shifted their focus back to me. Good. "How did you find me?"

"My grandad told me about a vet and some pit bull rescuer stopping by his house yesterday and nosing around about me." He kept the gun aimed at Parker. "Your vet buddy gave him a freaking card. I didn't have to look too hard to find you."

The blood drained from my face. "Ryan? Did you hurt him?"

"I'm asking the questions, not you. I'm in charge here."

Parker had used their focus on me to position himself by the driver side door of his truck. He'd been so quiet in his movements that I hadn't even noticed until I glanced back to check on him. I quickly directed my gaze back to Larry and his gang so I wouldn't give Parker's location away.

I heard sirens from a few miles away. Buzz had called

the cops. There wasn't a lot of cover between my road and the highway. As soon as Larry and his cronies heard the sirens, he might try to do something idiotic, like shoot us or take a hostage.

I hoped Parker could see me as I raised my hand up and turned a circle in the air to indicate police lights.

"Hey, where'd that other guy go?" Shotgun Bro #1 asked.

Great. The Bros noticed Parker was no longer a sitting duck.

"He was on your side," said Shotgun Bro #2.

The sirens got louder, but they were still minutes away. Even so, I took a small amount of pleasure at seeing the panic on Larry's face. This dumb jerk hadn't thought the situation through. "Did you really think we wouldn't call the police?"

The wheels were spinning in the country gangster's addled brain. Did he run or fight? I was hoping he'd run. I'd much rather the police take the fight to him than have the battle play out in my yard. "You should go," I said, encouragingly. "Better to run away and live to fight another day."

I could see Larry on the verge of making the rational decision to leave. But what he nor I expected, though I should of, was Nadine's resistance to being pushed aside in a crisis. My cop BFF went into full-scale deputy destroyer as she ran out of the house with her gun out in front of her. "Drop the weapons! Now," she said with a tone of pure authority.

Shotgun Bro #1 used a few choice expletives followed by, "It's the chick cop from the other day."

Larry's gun fired. I'm not sure if it was on purpose or by

mistake, but I felt the wind of the bullet slice past me. My eyes flashed as my cougar surged forward, ready to eat Larry's freaking face off. Nadine shot in his direction, her bullet ripping into his leg. Larry cried out. Bro #2 got off a shot as Parker, holding a tire iron, launched himself at him. I breathed a sigh of relief as the buckshot went wide.

I ran and leaped over the Pontiac to take down Bro #1, punching him in the face several times more than absolutely necessary.

More gunfire echoed. I heard a menacing roar as a giant cougar put himself between Nadine and Larry. Crap. It only took his mate being in danger to get him to shift. But now, the cops were almost at my driveway. Buzz couldn't be here as an animal. He had to change back. Now.

"Nadine!"

She looked at me, her eyes wide and terrified at blood-soaked Buzz's furry chest.

Oh, Goddess. He'd taken the hit. "Get him in the house," I hissed. "He has to change back."

"How?" she asked. Buzz wouldn't stop pacing back and forth, ready for whatever threatened Nadine next.

"Just go. He'll follow you." I breathed a sigh of relief when she started running to the porch, and Buzz followed. He hadn't shifted in so long. Was he strong enough to survive a bullet to the chest? I prayed it was so.

Larry was on his butt, scooting back. He still had his pistol and was waving it around. "Parker! Get down!" I yelled.

Deputies Gary Hall and Deb Morton were the first ones out of their cars, and I could tell Hall was wondering who the bad guys were as he looked back and forth from Parker to the men on the ground.

"It's them," I shouted as I took a position behind Parker's truck. "The guy on the ground there still has a loaded gun."

Deb Morton unholstered her service revolver. "Stay calm and tell me where?"

I was calm, practically Zen, considering the circumstances.

I pointed to where Larry had been a few seconds earlier, and the slippery son of a dog abuser had dragged himself behind his Pontiac.

A shot rang out again. Then I watched Deputy Morton empty her gun into Larry Johnson's chest.

I heaved a breath, gulping air as I tried to not hyperventilate.

"It's over." Parker held me. We both were shell-shocked. And just as I was his comfort stone, he was mine.

I nodded, but I didn't let him go. "We have to check on Buzz."

"Deb!" I heard Gary shout. He grabbed his radio from his vest and said, "Christ. We need an ambulance. Officer down," he said. "I repeat. Officer down."

CHAPTER 17

Thank the Goddess, Buzz shifted back to human before the ambulances arrived. The bullet had penetrated his shoulder, and I'd doubled up kitchen towels to make a pressure bandage to stop his bleeding. I didn't know how fast or slow he'd heal since he was a lot older than me on the one hand, but on the other, his lack of shifting had extolled a price from his body. Fortunately, the projectile looked to have missed any nerves or arteries.

Deb Morton hadn't gotten so lucky. Larry Johnson's shot angled upward into her lower abdomen, right below the bottom of her bulletproof vest. The first ambulance took her while we waited on the second one called for Buzz.

"You fool," Nadine cried. "You stupid old fool." She brushed at the tears on her cheek. "I swear to God if you knocked me up only to leave me alone to raise three hellions by myself, I will never forgive you."

"I'm going to be fine, honey. I promise. It's a minor

injury." He winced as she added extra pressure over the wound.

"I'm a police officer. You should've let me do my job. Putting babies in me doesn't give you the right to rule my life. I am not looking, nor am I asking for a hero." Nadine glared at me next. "This goes for you, too. I'm not some kitten that needs to be coddled. Do you guys get me? This keep-Nadine-in-the-dark bull crap and throwing yourself in front of bullets has got to stop."

"In my defense, I've only thrown myself in front of a bullet for you one time," Buzz said, then winced again when Nadine pressed harder.

"It's instinct," I told her. "You're carrying the next and only members of our blood. It's ingrained in our shifter DNA to protect the cubs." As I said it, I realized it was true. Buzz and I, until these babies, were the only two left of our family. Were we overcompensating because of that? Were we taking away Nadine's freedom to choose the way she wanted to live in the process? "I'm sorry, Nadine. I love you. But I never want to make you feel like you're weak or helpless."

She smiled at me. "Thanks, Lils. I appreciate you saying so. I forgive you, and I love you right back."

"I'm sorry too, honey," Buzz said.

"Shut up, Buzz," she snapped. "When this is all over, you better tell me everything you've been keeping from me, and I swear if you hold anything back, I'm going to shoot you in your other shoulder."

The second ambulance arrived, much to Buzz's relief. I

didn't think he'd survive Nadine's brand of caregiving for much longer.

We decided Parker would stay home with the dogs. Nadine rode in the ambulance with Buzz, and I followed in my truck. In all the chaos of the shootings, I'd forgotten about Ryan. I hit his number on speed dial and put him on speaker.

He picked up on the first ring. "Hey, Lily," he answered. "What's up?"

I burst into tears. I'd been holding back the dread of what Larry might have done to Ryan to get my information, that the relief at his benign greeting broke the dam wide open.

"Talk to me," Ryan said. "Are you hurt? Where are you? I'll come get you right now."

"I'm fine," I said when I could finally speak. I wiped the tears blurring my eyes. "Larry Johnson found me. Buzz's been shot. I'm following the ambulance to the hospital right now."

"How serious?"

"Shoulder. Not a through in through. He'll have to have the bullet surgically removed." And after, if his shifter mojo was working again, he'd heal in a couple of days. Dang it. I had to call Reggie. She needed to be his surgeon. "I'm going to call Reggie. Larry got my information from his grandpa, so I wanted to make sure you're okay. I'm happy you are."

"I'll call Mr. Johnson and make sure he's okay."

"Good idea," I said. "I'll talk to you tomorrow."

"Call me if you need anything."

"I will. Thanks, Ryan." I hung up on him and hit Reggie's number.

She picked up on the first ring. "I'm on my way to the hospital right now. Greer is on his way to your place to stay with Parker."

"Parker called." I blew out a relieved breath. Of course, he had. He was as good at taking care of me as I was at taking care of him.

"How are you doing?" she asked.

"I'm...better now." Ryan was alive and unharmed, Nadine was angry but safe, Parker and the dogs were healthy and in one piece, and Buzz would survive.

*****

By the time I arrived at the hospital, Ryan called to let me know Mr. Johnson was fine. Larry had threatened him but hadn't roughed him up. I parked in the emergency room parking lot and raced inside. They'd already taken Buzz back and were preparing him for surgery. I stopped at the check-in desk.

"Lily Mason," I said. "I'm here for Buzz Mason."

"We don't have a Buzz Mason checked in," she said looking at her computer.

"Daniel," I told her. "His real name is Daniel. He goes by Buzz."

"Here we are," she said. "Are you family?"

"Yes." I worried she wouldn't let me in if I said I was his cousin, and he looked too young to be my dad, so I added, "He's my brother." And in many ways, he was. Not a replacement for Danny, of course. More like an older sibling. I sometimes wondered how different our lives would have been if Buzz had been around when my parents died. Would he have stepped up to take care of Danny? I wasn't sure, but I wanted to believe it was true.

"I'll ring you back," she said. "Just wait at the double door there, and when the light turns green, you can go."

I nodded. Soon as the light changed, I pushed through and beelined it around the nurses' station. I recognized one of the nurses, Becky Thompson, doing paperwork at the desk. She'd been on duty the last time I'd been sent to the E.R. "Do you know where they took Buzz Mason? He was shot."

She looked over at the screen and typed in GSW. "In Exam Room 4," she said.

I was booking it across to four when she said, "Wait."

I didn't. Instead, I charged inside the room. However, it wasn't Buzz on the bed. It was Deb Morton. She had a team of medical professionals working around her, poking, sticking needles in her, setting up an EKG monitor.

"You need to step out," a woman said to me, as a doctor ordered, "Tell the O.R. we need a bed now."

Deb's shirt had been removed, and her stomach was exposed. My shoulders pinched as I tensed. Above Deb's pressure bandage was a long, thick scar stretching from one side of her abdomen to the other. She had been sliced open at some point in the past, and the scar reminded me of the slash across Rowdy's belly.

"Get out," the woman ordered again.

A million things raced through my mind as I stumbled back, fumbled the door handle, and almost fell onto my butt in the hallway. But there was one overriding thought that I couldn't shake. Deb Morton was somehow involved in Rowdy's death. I just wasn't sure how. Yet.

"I tried to tell you," Becky said frantically. "I gave you the wrong room. Mason is in Exam Room 1."

I rushed to Buzz's room and found him reclined on the hospital bed with a serene look on his face. Nadine sat next to him, holding his hand. It looked like she'd finally decided to forgive him too.

"Lily," he said, his voice slurred. "I love and appreciate you so sooooo much." He flopped his head to the side to look at Nadine. "And this one...ain't she boot...uhm, brut, no, that's not right." He snapped his fingers. "Beautiful. That's the word I wanted. Isn't she?"

"They've got him on morphine," Nadine said dryly as a way of explanation. "He's not feeling any pain right now."

"I'm glad. Reggie is on the way. She's going to do his surgery," I said. "And there's something else." I shook my head. "I think I know who took the missing knife."

She leaned forward but kept ahold of Buzz's hand. "Who?"

"Deb Morton."

Nadine shook her head. "No way. Deb Morton is as straight as they come. No way she tampered with evidence at a crime scene."

"How long have you known her?"

"Six maybe seven years. Deb has been with the sheriff's department as long as I have. She's a good cop, Lily."

I wanted to believe Nadine, but I couldn't shake the feeling that there was something all wrong about Deputy

Morton. "Do you know how she got the scar on her stomach?"

"Oh." Nadine tucked her chin. "Yeah." She looked away for a moment, trying to access the memory. "Deb told me she was in some kind of car accident when she was in college. I can't remember exactly. She got her associates in criminal justice at Two Hills Community College."

That didn't sound likely. The scar was thick but not jagged. It was basically a straight line from one side to the other. I didn't know how that kind of precision would happen in an automobile accident. "Is Deb from Moonrise?"

"I don't think so," Nadine said. "She's around my age. I would've remembered her from high school. Why are you sure it was Deb?"

"She went up to the house before the crime techs arrived. She was in the basement alone. And the scar on her stomach is remarkably similar to the wound I saw on Rowdy. It could all be a coincidence, but I don't think so."

Nadine nodded. "I'll see if I can find out more about Deb's past."

I had my own source I could ask about Deputy Morton. Kelly. She and I were both working tomorrow morning, and I'd see if she might have any information that could prove or disprove my theory. "I have a potential source," I said. "I'll see if I can find out anything pertinent."

Nadine's eyes narrowed a bit. "Who is this source, and is this source dangerous?"

"I can't tell you. Not unless it's necessary for the case. And no, I am not putting myself in danger."

"Fine." She sighed as she slid down in her chair, her butt

nearly off as she tried to relieve pressure in her back. "You should go home. There's no sense in hanging around. The doctor said Buzz was stable."

"Are you sure you don't want me here?"

"I'm sure." She waved wearily at me, the fatigue setting in. "Go home, Lily. I'll call you when he's out of surgery."

I put my purse down, grabbed a chair from the wall, and put it next to Nadine's. I sat down and took her free hand. "How about you hold his hand through this, and I'll hold yours."

Nadine's eyes misted over. "I could've lost him tonight."

"I know. Me too."

"Thanks, Lily." She leaned her head on my shoulder. "Thanks for being here."

I squeezed her hand. "That's what family is for."

CHAPTER 18

The next morning, I ambled into work at Petry's Pet Clinic at twelve minutes past eight o'clock. I'd never been late before, but I was operating on an hour of sleep and no coffee. Buzz's surgery went well. Reggie had been able to remove the bullet completely. And since it hadn't done more than some minor muscle damage, she was confident he'd get to come home today. I'd called Freda and Leon, and they both agreed to cover for Buzz for a few days until he could get back to the grill. And once Buzz was settled in on the recovery floor, it was after three in the morning.

Needless to say, it'd been a long night, and the morning wasn't getting any shorter.

"Morning, Lily," Abby said. "Did that man get ahold of you?"

"What man?" I asked.

"The one who was looking to adopt a pit bull."

"Was this yesterday?"

"Why, yes," she said. "He called right before closing."

I stifled a groan. That's how Larry Johnson knew my name. "Did you tell him where I lived?"

"Land sakes, no. But I did give him your shelter's contact information." She must have read my face because her smile faded. "I didn't do something wrong, did I?"

"No, Abby. You didn't." Larry was the only one in the wrong here. And now, he was dead. I rubbed my eyes. "Is Ryan in surgery already?"

"Yes," she answered. "Are you doing okay? You look awfully tired. I'm sure Dr. Petry could handle today without you."

"My cousin Buzz had to have emergency surgery." I didn't want to go into more detail because I liked Abby, and I didn't want her to feel responsible. I was certain if it hadn't been her giving Larry the information, it would've been someone else. He'd been determined to find me. I was just glad she hadn't thought to make any off-hand remarks about Elinor and Edward. "I'll be fine. I just need some caffeine."

Kelly was lingering by the coffee pot, her eyes swollen, and her usually bouncy curls were frizzy and messy. In other words, she resembled the way I felt.

We all kept personal coffee cups at the office to cut down on paper waste. I took mine from the rack and poured myself a cup. "I guess you heard, huh?"

"I don't know how she's doing. I don't know if she even survived her surgery."

"You should go to the hospital," I said.

"I can't." Kelly shook her head. "Deb made me promise.

She made me swear that if she was ever injured on the job that I wouldn't come. She said there would be people to help her from the sheriff's department and the community because that's what happens when an officer is injured on the job."

She looked so forlorn, I hugged her.

"I promised her," Kelly whispered as she hugged me back, then moved to the sink to grab a tissue from the box there. She blew her nose. "It wasn't like we were serious. It's only been a few months."

"It took me all of about two minutes to know I loved Parker," I said. I grabbed my phone from my purse. Bobby Morris picked up on the first ring.

"I've meant to call you, Lily, but I figured you were sleeping in."

"Can't," I said. "Had to work."

"Terrible business about last night. I suppose you know what I'm going to say next..."

"You need me to come down and make a statement."

"You were always a smart one."

I couldn't help myself. I laughed. Until I looked at Kelly's sad face again. "Hey, how's Deputy Morton doing? Did she come out of surgery okay?"

"She's in the ICU, but the surgeon says she's got a good shot at recovery, but it's a wait-and-see situation. You know how it goes." He paused. "I looked in on Buzz and Nadine this morning. I'm glad his injuries weren't more severe."

"If you gotta get shot, the shoulder is probably one of the better options."

Bobby chuckled. "You would know. You and Buzz will have matching scars now."

"I hadn't even thought of that." I'd been shot by a lunatic named Brigit Jones, no relation to the fictional character. Katherine Kapersky, her first victim, had been the local reverend's wife, the town council president, the choir leader, and a habitual blackmailer. I don't want to say she got what she deserved, but there had been more suspects than mourners when she'd been killed. I'd even had a nasty run-in or two with her, and I'd only been in town a day. Needless to say, I was tired of people shooting at me and the people I loved.

"Was there anything else you needed? I have an appointment with the mayor. My first official budget meeting as sheriff."

I smiled. "I wish you all the best." After I got off the phone, I took Kelly's hand. "She's in recovery, and it looks like she's going to be just fine."

This time Kelly hug-hugged me. "Thank you, Lily. I can't tell you how much—"

"And you don't have to." I gave her a quick pat. "Hey, if you think you love Deb, maybe you should tell her."

"I'm not ready to stop seeing her, yet." Kelly chuckled dryly as she dabbed her eyes. "She was pretty clear from the start that she only wanted a casual relationship. No strings attached."

"I'm convinced that there's no such thing as no strings attached," I said. "When we let people into our lives, for good or for ill, they become part of our story. There are always strings." I pushed down the guilt as I said, "and I bet it's more than casual for Deb. After all, the night Rowdy died, she went to you. You were the person she wanted to talk to the most, right?"

"You're right." She sighed. "She was pretty upset that night when she came over."

"Is Deb from Moonrise?" I already knew she wasn't from my discussion with Nadine, but I needed a jumping-off point.

"She's from Arkansas," Kelly said. "Somewhere near the Green Mountains. She moved to Moonrise for school."

I nodded. "Does Deb have any family back home? Maybe someone to notify?"

"The only person she still has any contact with is her cousin. I can't remember her name." Kelly squinted. "Actually, I don't think she ever said it. Her cousin was always in some trouble or another, but Deb loved her."

"Loved?"

"They had a falling out some years ago, but the way she talked about her cousin, I know Deb still loves her."

"Wow, for a no-strings relationship, she sure shared a lot of herself with you."

Kelly's eyes brightened. "I guess she did."

I pushed a little truth juju into my next words. "I was at the hospital last night, and I saw a scar on her stomach. Do you know what that's from?" Nice, I thought to myself, zero subtlety. But seriously, how do you work an abdominal scar into a conversation?

Kelly averted her gaze. "She doesn't talk about it." She closed her eyes as if reliving a painful moment. "The first time I touched it, she flinched away. I think someone hurt her."

"Not a car accident?"

"Not that she ever said." She tapped her chin. "Although, she did let it slip once that she used to take ballet when she was young. She said she used to love to dance. But then something happened, and she told me she never wanted to dance again. Maybe it was a car accident."

Goddess, so much for keeping it casual. Regardless, it sounded like there was more to the story about her stomach scar than what she'd told Nadine.

*****

After my shift was over, I headed to the hospital. I knew in my head that Buzz was okay, but my heart was a "see for yourself" kind of gal. I felt bad for Kelly. She'd fallen in love with Deb Morton. However, Kelly deserved someone open about who she was and emotionally available. I didn't think Deb was that person on either account.

When I arrived, Buzz was sitting up on the edge of his bed, dressed and ready to go. "Where's Nadine?" I asked.

"She's going to find a nurse and a wheelchair so I can get the hell out of here," he said.

"Daaang. What happened to...," I gave my best approximation of Buzz on drugs, "I loooove yooo and appprecccciate you so much."

"Very funny," he said. He scrubbed his hand over his face. "If I ever get shot again, don't let them give me morphine."

"If you ever get shot again, they're going to have to give me morphine." I crossed the room and gently put my arms around him so I wouldn't aggravate his shoulder. "Thank you."

"For what?"

"For putting yourself in front of Nadine. For surviving. You name it." The last few days had really stirred up my feelings about love, loss, and family. Grief had a funny way of disappearing for long periods of time, then sneaking back up on you and whacking you upside the head when you least expected it.

"You're welcome," he replied. "For all of the above."

I narrowed my gaze on him and kept my tone hushed. "You shifted."

"I did." He nodded.

"Can you do it again?"

He showed me his hand. I watched as reddish-brown fur covered the area and claws replaced his nails. "I can." Steps down the hallway prompted him to withdraw his cougar. "I think you were right. All my fears about losing Nadine and our children," he shook his head, "it had made me a coward. But seeing Nadine in danger destroyed whatever was blocking me from shifting."

"Pressure cooker exploded," I said.

He grinned. "Yep, pressure cooker went boom."

The door opened. "Good, Lily. You're here," Nadine said. She was pushing a wheelchair. "You can help me spring Buzz."

"Isn't a nurse supposed to do that?"

"I'm tired of waiting around for one." She patted the seat. "This place is for sick people, and as you can plainly see, Buzz is not a sick person."

"Did you steal a wheelchair?"

"It's not stealing if you plan to give it back."

"That's not technically true. Borrowing without asking is still stealing."

Nadine frowned at me. "Then you better arrest me, Deputy Lily."

I waved a hand dismissively. "No, thank you. What's the hurry?"

Nadine spoke between clenched teeth. "His shoulder is healed."

"Really?" It had taken me three days for the bullet wound in my shoulder to heal. Buzz had barely been out of surgery for twelve hours. "Did someone see?"

"A wound specialist. He went to go get a doctor, and I want to get out of here before they get back and..."

"And what?" I moved my gaze from Nadine to Buzz. "You told her your fears about government men finding out about us and taking us to be experimented on, didn't you?" That was one of the first talks that Buzz had given me about integrating into the human world. If the humans found out about us, they would turn us into lab rats to see what made us tick.

He shrugged. "Are you saying it's not true?"

"I'm saying this pregnancy is making you both crazy," I shot back.

"I'm not taking any chances." Nadine shoved the wheelchair over. "Get in, Buzz."

Buzz stood up. "I can walk out."

"Then why did you send me to get a wheelchair?"

"You needed something to do," he said.

"Until what?" she asked.

Reggie walked in with a handful of paperwork. "Here's your discharge orders, all signed and ready to go." She gave Nadine a baleful gaze. "If you don't want people to ask questions, then don't behave suspiciously. Besides, insurance won't pay the bill if you leave the hospital against medical advice. You don't want to be saddled with surgery bills right now. Not with triplets on the way."

"I have hormones enough to make three whole freaking human beings inside my body. My boobs hurt, I've been throwing up for months, my ankles are swollen, and my emotions are raw," tears crested her eyes, "and this morning, I noticed a weird rash on my thighs. Acting suspicious is the least of my worries."

"I'll write you a prescription for the rash," Reggie said.

A nurse knocked on the door then entered with a wheelchair when Reggie told her to come in. "Oh, you already have a wheelchair," she said.

Nadine flushed but didn't confess.

Reggie smiled. "I leave you in the capable hands of Sonya here." She indicated the nurse. "Sonya, I've already gone over the discharge orders with Mr. Mason. He just needs a ride out of the building." She gave Nadine a meaningful look. "Hospital orders."

I stepped out of the room with Reggie. "Boy, Nadine is on edge."

"She's not wrong about hormones doing a number on the body and the brain. I think she's remarkably sane, all things considered." She shoved her hand in her pocket. "Walk with me."

"What's up?" I asked.

"I got the toxicology reports back from the lab on Ronald Dawson."

"What did you find?"

"Rohypnol," she said.

"The date rape drug?"

"Yep. It would have made the victim confused and compliant."

That accounted for the lack of defensive wounds and signs of restraints. "So, Dawson would have had enough Rohypnol in him for someone to slice his stomach and shove money down his throat without any real kind of struggle."

"Exactly."

We rounded the corner of the recovery ward. Gary Hall was standing outside in the hallway, talking on his cell."

"We need to talk to Deb Morton." I pointed up ahead. "Is that her room?"

"I don't know. She's not my patient."

And then Gary Hall said something that stopped me in my tracks. "Yes, sir. Deputy Morton has made a full confession."

CHAPTER 19

After Hall asked Reggie for a copy of the toxicology report, she left for her basement office next to the morgue. He wanted to corroborate Deb Morton's confession about drugging Rowdy. There was a deputy outside of Deb's door as several uniformed officers went in and out of the room. Which meant there was no way I was getting in to see Deb now. She'd confessed to killing Rowdy, but I didn't understand how that was possible. She'd responded to the call. Wouldn't her partner question the timeline?

Bobby was talking to Deputy Hall, but there was too much chaos for me to hear what they were saying. Hall had asked me to stick around to answer a few questions, and since I wanted some answers, I didn't argue with him. After a short while, Bobby waved me over.

"Lily, Deputy Hall says you saw a knife in the basement the night Ronald Dawson was killed."

I gave the young, ambitious deputy an appraising glance. He'd been startled when I'd mentioned the knife in my witness statement, but I hadn't thought much of it at the time. "I did."

Gary Hall held up his phone to show me a photo. "Is this the knife you saw?"

The opened-blade knife in the photo had a black handle and looked exactly like the one I'd seen in the spilled litter. Only, without the blood. "It's the same kind of knife," I said. "It's just like the one I saw that night. Where did you find it?"

He nodded. "Hidden in a vent in the home of Kelly Spenser."

I felt the keen sting of betrayal for Kelly. Deb Morton had used her lover's home as a place to hide key evidence. And while we weren't close outside of work, I realized that I did think of Kelly as a friend. "Why would she do that?"

"She says she accidentally dropped the knife when Darren Larson arrived on the scene. She'd escaped out the back door. Drove back to Moonrise and checked into her shift."

"But how did she catch the call?"

Bobby shook his head. "She made the call herself, using Rowdy's phone when we stopped at a gas station at the beginning of our shift. Then she got rid of it. We found the phone in the Quick and Go bathroom."

I was still struggling to buy it. "How about Rowdy's truck? Darren said he saw Rowdy arrive in it on the camera."

"We couldn't salvage the video enough to determine the vehicle. And Deb does drive a dark blue SUV," Gary added.

"I'm sorry, Lily." Bobby placed his hand on my shoulder. "I know Parker's friend had to endure a lot the past few days, but we were operating with the evidence we were given."

I looked at Gary. "You were suspicious of your partner? Why?"

"You were sure there was a knife, and Deb had gone back into the house alone for several minutes." Gary shook his head. "Even so, I didn't want to believe it could be her. But then she was shot. I saw her stomach." Maybe Deputy Hall would eventually make a good cop or even an FBI agent. He'd followed the evidence, wherever it led.

"The scar," I filled in the blank.

"It seemed like too big of a coincidence."

"She confessed to all of this?" I asked.

Bobby nodded. "She did."

"Did she say why?"

Gary answered. "She only gave us the how. Whatever her motivation, she doesn't want us to know."

"We'll have to be satisfied that justice is done," Bobby said. "The charges are being dropped against Parker's friend, of course."

"That'll make for some good news, at least."

Gary met my gaze, then averted his eyes. "Can I talk to you for a moment?"

I nodded and followed him aside.

He toed the tile, leaving a scuff mark behind. "I'm sorry, Ms. Mason, for pulling my weapon on you the other night. I'd been wound tight since..." He shook his head. "It's no excuse. I just wanted you to know that I'm sorry."

"Deputy Hall, I think you're probably a fine police officer, but I'm going to tell you something that you probably don't want to hear. You're not always going to know who the bad guys are, but if you go around seeing everyone as a potential threat, then you become a threat to everyone." I tried to soften my words. "Just something to think about."

He didn't argue with me, which raised him even more in my esteem.

There were enough clues to make Deb Morton the plausible murderer, with the confession being the biggest clue of all. However, I still felt like there were pieces missing from her story.

As I walked down the hall, I retrieved my phone to call Parker. I had two missed text messages from Mia, so I called her first.

"Lily, thank heavens," she said. "Did you hear? They are dropping all the charges against Darren."

"That's great news," I replied.

"I can't tell you how thankful I am to you for all your help."

"I didn't do much," I said, still unable to fight the niggling feeling that I was missing something.

"You really helped Darren the other night. I've never seen him open up so fast to anyone."

"I'm glad I could help."

"I was hoping you could do me one more favor."

"If I can."

"Can you find out from your friend, Dr. Crawford, when I can get Rowdy? I'm ready to put my brother to rest now."

I understood more than anyone how she was feeling. Rowdy had been a burden she took on after the loss of her parents, and she had loved and cared for him even when he might have been less than lovable. Putting him to rest would be her final duty for her brother. Only then would she be able to move on.

At least that's how it had been for me.

"I'll go talk to her right now," I said. "I'll get back to you as soon as I know something."

****

The basement of the hospital always creeped me out. The narrow hallways bounced sound around as if you were standing in a crypt. The floor was mostly used for storage and maintenance, except for the morgue and Reggie's office. The rest of the space was reserved for underground parking. The last time I'd been here, I'd chased a killer into the parking garage, where she'd proceeded to run me over. Unlucky for her, I don't damage easily.

Reggie's office was empty when I arrived, so I checked the morgue next. I heard her say, "I wish I could help you."

"That's okay, Doc. I just wanted to see him one last time," a woman said. I recognized the voice. It was Racine.

I knocked, then entered. "Hey, Reggie. Everything okay?"

Racine's eyes were puffy and red-rimmed. She'd been crying. Had the grief of Rowdy's death pushed through her anger at him? Even in a breakup, feelings didn't simply disappear.

"Ms. Little wanted to say goodbye to Ronald Dawson. I was just explaining that I can't hold a viewing for non-family members."

"It's fine," Racine said. "I don't want to cause any problems. I'll just go."

Reggie's expression softened with sympathy. "The

autopsy is completed. It won't hurt anything to give you a minute with him. You should get to say goodbye."

I walked with Reggie over to a low cooler door. "Hey, I've actually come to see when Rowdy's sister can pick him up. To make funeral arrangements and such."

"Like I told Ms. Little, I'm done with my part." She smiled sadly. "Tell his sister that we'll coordinate with whatever funeral home she chooses to get his body transferred."

"Thanks."

Reggie opened the door and slid a steel table holding, I assumed, Rowdy, beneath a sheet. She folded the sheet down just far enough to expose his face, then stepped back. "Ms. Little," she said. "I can only give you a minute, okay?"

Racine sniffed, then nodded once. "I won't need any more time than that."

Her lithe frame was graceful, a dancer's body, as she strolled over. Reggie and I took a few steps away to give her some space.

"You know," she said, her voice choked. "I didn't think he'd look so...waxy." She sighed.

It was an odd observation, but I knew that pain and loss could manifest in different people different ways.

"You hurt people," she hissed. "You hurt someone I loved dearly. Don't get me wrong, there were times I actually enjoyed your stupid ass. And that just makes me all the more sickened."

"Okay," Reggie said. "Maybe we should wrap this up."

Tears were hot in Racine's eyes as she turned toward us. She had a small pistol aimed in our direction.

Reggie let out a squeak of surprise.

I growled, fighting the urge to react, but Goddess help me, I was tired of all these yahoos pointing their guns at me. "Please, put that away," I said. "You don't want to do this."

"Believe me, I do. Twenty-two dollars," she said. "That's how much it cost me to lose my family. Twenty-two lousy dollars. All because I'd told her how easy the money was for exotic dancing. You do a few parties, earn a lot of pay. No big deal. She was struggling with college debt. I thought I was helping." A sob escaped her. "She was only nineteen, and she trusted me." She swiped at her eyes with her free hand. "It was a bachelor party. I'd done a dozen of them before. You get a few hundred bucks for taking your top off, and it's over." She shook her head jerkily. "She barely survived the blood loss. In the hospital, she'd told me that she hadn't been able to move. She could hear them, feel them, but she couldn't fight them. And they just kept saying they were going to get their money's worth." Her voice caught on another sob. "What kind of monsters do that?"

"Deb Morton's your cousin," I said. My stomach knotted as I thought about what she must have gone through.

"They ruffied her drink, then they did terrible things to her. She never told a soul what happened. Except me. They threw twenty-two one-dollar bills onto her when they were done, then left her to die. I'd found her unconscious. She didn't want to press charges. She wanted to forget and leave the past behind. I was part of that past." She pressed the handle of the gun against her temple. "I just wanted to scare him. I wanted him to feel what she must've felt. I didn't mean for Deb..."

"You put those bills down his throat even after he was dead," I said. "That's not an accident."

"Shut up," Racine snapped. "Just shut up." She aimed the pistol in my direction. "She saw me out with Rowdy on a date one night. Can you imagine?"

"You didn't know he was one of the men who raped her?"

Racine shook her head. "He had money. We had fun. How could I know?"

"And then she told you the truth about your boyfriend." I stepped closer to her. I couldn't outrun a bullet, but I might be able to get to her before she could get a shot off.

Reggie's hand fidgeted nervously in her pocket. "I know what it's like to be with a no-good bastard," Reggie said. "I was married to one for sixteen years before I got away."

"Don't try to connect with me, lady." Racine rolled her eyes. "This isn't a negotiation."

"Then what is it?" Reggie asked.

I inched closer still.

"It's my suicide note," Racine replied. "I killed Rowdy Dawson. It was me and me alone. Debra Morton is only guilty of hiding my knife. I knew about the cameras. I disabled them and got rid of them on my own. I'm not sorry he's dead, and if given a chance, I track down every single one of those sons of bitches and kill them too."

She lifted the gun and pressed the barrel to her heart. "Tell Deb I'm sorry. Tell her..." She stared off into the distance for a moment, and I sprang the remaining distance between us and tackled Racine to the ground.

Bobby Morris and Gary Hall rushed as I smashed her gun hand on the tile. She let go, and I slapped it away.

I focused my attention on Racine. "You can tell Deb yourself," I said. "You'll have plenty of time to make amends in prison."

"We got here as soon as I got Dr. Crawford's text," Bobby said. He walked over and took possession of the weapon. "Are you two all right?"

I got up. Gary took Racine into custody. "She's the one who killed Rowdy," I told him. "She's Deb's cousin. She's got a story to tell."

If Hall was half as tenacious as I thought he was, this wasn't the end of the investigation. It was only the beginning.

Reggie crossed the room to me. "I feel sorry for her," she said. "Is it immoral to wish a man dead twice over?"

"If it is, then we are both immoral." I shook my head. "When and how did you text Bobby?"

"He'd sent me a message earlier, so it was a matter of opening my phone and sending him a message back."

"But how? You never had your phone out."

She patted her lab coat pocket. "You don't raise a teenage girl without learning how to blind text someone."

CHAPTER 20

"They love each other!" Reggie squealed.

I laughed as Smooshie, Elvis, Elinor, and Edward, raced around Reggie's backyard. Parker, Buzz, and Greer stood out in the freshly fallen snow to make sure that the playing didn't turn into something else.

"Where do you want these stockings hung?" Nadine asked.

"On the mantle," Reggie said. "Duh." She looked outside again. "Awww. You need to get yourself some fur babies, Nadine. I didn't know how much I needed them until they were here."

"I'm going to have baby-babies. Besides, I already have a fur baby, and his name is Buzz," Nadine replied.

Reggie laughed. "That's fair."

After the awfulness of the past week, we'd spent the past three days getting Greer moved into Reggie's place. I guess it was Greer's place now, too. He looked good, younger. He'd never forget Parker's mom. He'd mourned her loss for a long time, but he was letting go of the past and embracing his future.

Deb Morton was still in the hospital and would need rehabilitation for months to come. The first person she'd wanted to see when the news about her cousin unfolded was Kelly. I wasn't sure if Kelly would forgive her for hiding evidence at her house, but there was no telling when it came to matters of the heart.

Deb would lose her job as a deputy for tampering with evidence and conspiracy to cover up a crime. Still, considering her past service and the circumstances surrounding the crime, I believed the district attorney would offer her a plea deal. Maybe she could start over. Maybe with Kelly. I hoped so, anyhow.

Racine Little made a full confession and showed no remorse. Her sentencing remained to be seen, but I didn't think she'd spend another Christmas outside of prison for a very long time. In a way, I think she wanted to be punished. She blamed herself for what had happened to Deb. I hoped one day she could let go of her past. Living with constant blame, guilt, and recrimination was no life at all.

"Come on, people," Nadine snapped. "These decorations won't put themselves up."

"How cool would that be, though? Like, if we just went to bed and elves did their thing overnight, and bing, boom, bam." Reggie dusted her palms. "Magical Christmas."

"If elves broke into my house in the middle of the night, I'd shoot them," Nadine said.

I groaned on a laugh. "Haven't we had enough shootings for one week?"

"For a lifetime," Reggie agreed.

"I'm kidding." Nadine grabbed some candles from a box marked centerpiece. "I wouldn't shoot them. Instead, I'd put them in tiny handcuffs and arrest them all for trespassing."

"You're a mean one, Mister Grinch," I said.

"That's Ms. Grinch," she corrected. Then she laughed. "Actually, I am looking forward to Christmas this year." She shrugged. "I'm not nauseated anymore, thanks to Doc Miracle over here," she gestured to Reggie, "and Buzz is back to his old self. It makes me optimistic."

"You should be. It's going to be a wonderful New Year," I told her and prayed it wasn't wishful thinking. "Is CeCe excited to come home for the holiday break?" I asked Reggie.

"I don't know. I think she is." Reggie bit her lower lip. "She's bringing home a new boyfriend. I don't know how I feel about it."

"You'll hate him, I'm sure," I said.

Nadine and I both laughed. Reggie wasn't amused.

Family. This past week had sent me down memory lane. Some of it was good, some not so much. I never doubted my feelings for Parker or his feelings for me, but this week had emphasized how important it was for me to show him that I valued our life together above everything else.

"Do you have champagne?" I asked Reggie.

"Does the Pope wear a hat?" she replied.

I was pretty sure he did. "Wonderful."

"What are we toasting?" Nadine put down the candles and leaned over the breakfast bar.

"I've got sparkling cider for you," Reggie said, then turned to me. "But to her point, what are we celebrating?"

"Just wait and see." I opened the door. "Will you guys come inside for a minute?"

Smooshie ran past me, Elinor on her heels. They slid across the tile, panting and wagging their wiggly butts in a way that made me so happy. Elvis and Edward, the more stoic of the dogs, walked in with the men.

They pounded their feet on the doormat to knock the snow off their boots before coming inside and taking them off. Parker hung up his coat, then wrapped his arms around me. He put his cold hands on my back, and I squirmed at the ice against my warm skin.

I tilted my head up and met his bright, blue gaze. The stocking cap he wore covered his dark brown hair, except for a few cute loose curls that had escaped the edges.

"What's up, babe?"

Goddess, this man made me happy. And I realized I'd do anything to make him happy. "Parker, I am yours, my heart, my body, and my soul. The way I love you is nothing that I ever thought or even hoped I could feel. And the way you love me makes me want to pinch myself every day so that I know I'm not dreaming."

He smiled as his eyes misted. "I'm yours, Lily. My body, my heart, my soul. I'd been lost for a long time until you found me, and with you, I always know how to find my way home."

Nadine coughed as she stifled a sob.

I glanced over at Buzz. "Will you seal us?"

Buzz walked over to the Christmas ornament box and

found a length of gold ribbon. He wrapped our hands together, finishing with a binding knot, an old tradition for a shifters' handfast ritual. He placed his hands above and below ours. "In the eyes of the Goddess and this gathering of family and friends, do you pledge to run together?"

"I do," I said.

Parker, who had no idea what the ritual was, had no problem jumping in. "I do," he said. His smile widened, and his eyes were glassy with emotion.

Buzz nodded. "Do you pledge to play together?"

"We do," we both said.

"Will you pledge to hunt together and never apart?"

"I do," we repeated.

"And do you pledge to love each other through sunshine and rain?"

I was crying now as we both said, "We do."

"Then, in the eyes of the Goddess and this gathering of family and friends, I declare you both mated for life."

Parker dipped his head and kissed me so tenderly, I wept. "I am your wife," I told him. "And you're my husband."

He nodded and pressed his forehead to mine.

"Are you happy?" I asked.

His voice was husky and thick with emotion. "The happiest."

The End

PARANORMAL MYSTERIES & ROMANCES

BY RENEE GEORGE

Nora Black Midlife Psychic Mysteries

www.norablackmysteries.com
Sense & Scent Ability (Book 1)
For Whom the Smell Tolls (Book 2)
War of the Noses (Book 3)
Aroma With A View (Book 4) (Coming Early 2021)

Peculiar Mysteries

www.peculiarmysteries.com
You've Got Tail (Book 1) FREE Download
My Furry Valentine (Book 2)
Thank You For Not Shifting (Book 3)
My Hairy Halloween (Book 4)
In the Midnight Howl (Book 5)
My Peculiar Road Trip (Magic & Mayhem) (Book 6)
Furred Lines (Book7)
My Wolfy Wedding (Book 8)
Who Let The Wolves Out? (Book 9)

Paranormal Mysteries & Romances

My Thanksgiving Faux Paw (Book 10)

Witchin' Impossible Cozy Mysteries
www.witchinimpossible.com
Witchin' Impossible (Book 1) FREE Download
Rogue Coven (Book 2)
Familiar Protocol (Booke 3)
Mr & Mrs. Shift (Book 4)

Barkside of the Moon Mysteries
www.barksideofthemoonmysteries.com
Pit Perfect Murder (Book 1) FREE Download
Murder & The Money Pit (Book 2)
The Pit List Murders (Book 3)
Pit & Miss Murder (Book 4)
The Prune Pit Murder (Book 5)
Two Pits and A Little Murder (Book 6)

Madder Than Hell
www.madder-than-hell.com
Gone With The Minion (Book 1)
Devil On A Hot Tin Roof (Book 2)
A Street Car Named Demonic (Book 3)

Hex Drive
https://www.renee-george.com/hex-drive-series
Hex Me, Baby, One More Time (Book 1)
Oops, I Hexed It Again (Book 2)
I Want Your Hex (Book 3)
Hex Me With Your Best Shot (Book 4)

Midnight Shifters
    www.midnightshifters.com
    Midnight Shift (Book 1)
    The Bear Witch Project (Book 2)
    A Door to Midnight (Book 3)
    A Shade of Midnight (Book 4)
    Midnight Before Christmas (Book 5)

SENSE AND SCENT ABILITY

A NORA BLACK MIDLIFE PSYCHIC MYSTERY
BOOK 1

My name is Nora Black, and I'm fifty-one years young. At least that's what I tell myself, when I'm not having hot flashes, my knees don't hurt, and I can find my reading glasses.

I'm also the proud owner of a salon called Scents & Scentsability in the small resort town of Garden Cove, where I make a cozy living selling handmade bath and beauty products. All in all, my life is pretty good.

Except for one little glitch...

Since my recent hysterectomy, where I died on the operating table, I've been experiencing what some might call paranormal activity. No, I don't see dead people, but quite suddenly I'm triggered by scents that, in their wake, leave behind these vividly intense memories. Sometimes they're unfocused and hazy, but there's no doubt, they are very, very real.

Know what else? They're not my memories. It seems I've lost a uterus and gained a psychic gift.

When my best friend's abusive boyfriend ends up dead after a fire, and she becomes the prime suspect, I end up a babysitter to her two teenagers while she's locked up in the clink. Add to that the handsome detective determined to stand in my way, my super sniffer's newly acquired abilities and a rash of memories connected to the real criminal, and I find myself in a race to catch a killer before my best friend is tried for murder.

Chapter One

"I think I have a brain tumor," I blurted as I flung open my front door for my best friend, Gillian "Gilly" Martin. She held a bottle of wine in one hand and a grocery bag filled with honey buns, potato chips, salted nuts, and chocolate-covered raisins in her other.

"You don't have a brain tumor." Gilly passed off the bag and the bottle, then brushed past me, shrugging off her coat and hanging it on the hall tree. It had been a cold March, with temperatures in the low 40s most days. Under the coat, Gilly wore a form-fitting, long-sleeved, baby blue turtleneck sweater and black palazzo pants that flared out over a pair of black flats. Her straight chestnut-brown hair was in a loose ponytail for our girls' night in.

"Are you pooping okay?" she asked. "The doctor said you weren't supposed to strain. You could pop internal stitches."

"Quit asking me about my bowel habits," I said. "As of yesterday, I've been cleared to resume normal activity. Like straining when I poop. Besides, I'm worried about my head, not my butt." After all, my mother had died of brain cancer. "I've been… " I trailed off, trying to find the right words. "Seeing things."

Gilly squeezed my shoulder in an effort to comfort me. "You had a hysterectomy, Nora. Didn't the doctor say you might feel strange for a while?"

Um…if strange included dying on the operating table and then discovering strong scent-induced hallucinations, then yeah. I felt strange. I mean if death was gonna bring me a gift, I would've liked something a lot more useful than the ability to smell other people's troubles.

How could I possibly explain my new weird ability to her? Well, obviously, I couldn't. It had been eight weeks since my surgery, and I still hadn't figured out a way to confide in Gilly.

"Nora?"

I sighed. "I need a drink." I lifted up the wine bottle. "Let me pop this sucker." Gilly still looked concerned, but I smiled and nodded toward the living room. "Be right there."

A few minutes later, I handed Gilly her glass of Cabernet Sauvignon and sat down next to her on the couch.

"You know, regular activities include sex," Gilly said with a little too much enthusiasm. She waggled her brows at me.

"Sex hasn't been a regular activity for me in a very long time." Two years to be exact. I wasn't a prude. It's just that there hadn't been a lot of opportunities. Between caring for my mother during the last stages of her illness and dealing with painful uterine fibroids, dating and sex were the last things I cared about.

"You are way too hot to be celibate."

"Sure." I patted my swelly-belly. "I've gained ten pounds in the last two months."

"You just had your guts cut out," she said with a fair amount of exasperation. Then she flashed me her signature Gilly Martin smile, and added, "Besides, men like women with curves."

I frowned and pinched some of my stomach fat. "It's too squishy to be a curve."

She laughed. "Girl. I got squishy curves all over." She rubbed her tummy. "Including my midsection." She fluffed her ponytail. "And I'm sexy as hell."

I grinned. "You certainly are." I had always lacked the confidence Gilly displayed about her looks and body. She wasn't wrong about her sex appeal. Men were drawn to her like bears to honey.

"Have I told you lately how happy I am that you're back in Garden Cove?"

I rolled my eyes then grinned. "All the time."

"I can't help it. I missed you when you lived in the city." Her sigh held a hint of sadness. "Though, I'm sorry for the reason you had to come home."

Last year, my mother's brain cancer had progressed to its final stage. My father had died ten years ago, and I was an only child. Mom only had me. So, I'd taken a compassionate leave of absence from work as a regional sales manager for a prominent health and beauty line to care for her. It had turned into an early retirement when my employer decided they wanted to keep my temporary replacement, a younger, more cutthroat version of myself. Thankfully, they'd offered me a generous severance package if I would go quietly, including covering medical insurance costs until I qualified for Medicare in fourteen years.

I'd accepted their offer. Spending time with Mom until her final moments had been a blessing. I didn't regret a minute of caring for her. Of course, from the hospice workers, the aides, the nurses, the volunteers who would sit with her while I shopped, and even the chaplain who brought her some spiritual comfort, I hadn't done it alone.

My mother had been the rock of our family, a major source of comfort and stability. When she got sick, she'd minimized the severity of her cancer because she hadn't wanted me to worry. Honestly, I'd believed she'd beat it. I'd never seen Mom not succeed when she put her mind to something. If only I had known how bad it really was, I would have come home sooner.

Reconnecting with Gilly had been one of the major bright spots since moving back to Garden Cove. We'd been inseparable during elementary and high school. She'd been the maid of honor at my wedding and had done the pub crawl up in the city with me when my divorce had finalized. I had been twenty-nine at the time. It was hard to believe that twenty-two years had passed since then. When I was in my teens, I couldn't wait for high school to be over so I could make my own life. Then in college, I couldn't wait to graduate so I could be married. Later, when my marriage fell apart, I couldn't wait to be out of it so I could move away from Garden Cove and start my career.

I'd spent so much time wishing my life away that I'd failed to really live in the moment. I didn't want to be that person anymore.

My whole life had been go-go-go, and I was ready for some slow-slow-slow.

I squeezed Gilly's hand. "I missed you, too. You know, it's not too late to quit your job and come work with me in the shop."

Gilly smiled. "I like running the spa at the Rose Palace Resort."

"I know you do." I didn't press her. We'd had this conversation a dozen times since I'd bought Tidwell's Diner and converted it into an apothecary, where I sold homemade beauty and aromatherapy products. I couldn't afford to pay her what she was worth, anyhow. But it didn't stop me from wishing we could spend more time together. I considered myself lucky that she'd had tonight free.

Gilly was a single mom to teenage twins, and the high school was out for their short spring break that would end on Monday and Tuesday thanks to snow days in January that they still had to make up. The kids were doing overnights at their friends, while Gilly had packed a bag to stay in my guest bedroom and leave for work in the morning from here. Hence the wine. "How are the kids doing?"

"Like they would tell me." Gilly snorted. "They're teenagers, so they share as little as possible. Marco seems to be doing okay. He's dating a girl a year older than him. A senior. Can you believe it? I wouldn't have ever dated a younger boy in high school."

"Marco's a good-looking kid."

"He's only sixteen and just like his dad," Gilly agreed. "Oozing charm and confidence. Worries me sometimes."

"He's not anything like Gio," I assured her. Marco, while moody and temperamental at times, had a kind heart, unlike his father, who only cared about himself. The twins never saw their dad anymore, and that was on Giovanni Rossi. After the divorce, he took a head chef position at an Italian restaurant in Vegas. He used his work as a way to avoid parental responsibility. Too often, Gilly carried that burden of guilt, as if it was her fault Gio had abandoned his kids.

"What about Ari?" I asked.

"She made the honor roll." Gilly's daughter's full name was Ariana Luna Isabelle Rossi. A beautiful name, but she preferred Ari. The girl marched to the beat of her own drum, and I loved that about her. Where her mother was hyper-feminine in both hair and clothes, Ari wore her hair like James Dean, and her outfits tended to be androgynous. "She's so smart, but I can't help but worry about her. She's so damned quiet. How in the world did I, a woman who can't shut up, raise a daughter who doesn't like to talk?"

"You got me there," I said, offering a sly smirk.

"Nora!" She smacked my arm. "You're terrible."

"Ouch." I rubbed the spot and laughed. "I really am. Good for Ari, though," I said. "She's always been a smart cookie. And her drive and ambition to excel will take her places." I didn't have children by choice, but that hadn't stopped me from agreeing to be Marco and Ari's godmother. When I lived in the city, I'd sent the kids packages every year for birthdays and Christmas, but I hadn't spent a lot of time with them until I returned to Garden Cove. "She's going to be just fine, even if she didn't inherit her mother's gift of gab." I slung my arm around Gilly's shoulders and squeezed, careful not to jostle our wine glasses.

I caught the sweet scent of raspberries with notes of citrus and vanilla.

Blurry shapes form...a woman stands in front of a large man who towers over her. Faces are hazy. It appears as if they're both made of colored smoke.

"It's over, Lloyd."

I recognize Gilly's voice.

"Don't be that way, Gilly," the man cajoles. "I didn't mean anything by it."

Gilly's voice chokes. "I really like you, but I can't be with someone who would say those things. Especially about my daughter. Ari is a great kid."

She turns away from him and he grabs her arm. Gilly gasps as he yanks her against his body.

"We belong together." He manacles both her wrists with his large hands. "You have to give me another chance."

"Get your hands off me," she says, pain evident in her shaking voice.

"I'll never let you go." His menacing tone chills me to the bone. "Never."

"Hello." Gilly snapped her fingers in front of my face. "Earth to Nora."

"What?" I said, blinking at my friend.

Her brow furrowed. "Are you okay?"

"You're going to get grooves between your eyes if you don't stop worrying about me." Although, at this point, I had enough worry for the both of us." "How is it going with the new guy you're dating? Lloyd Briscoll, right?"

Gilly went pale and the wine glass in her hand trembled. I took it from her, then placed both of our glasses on the coffee table. "Gilly?"

"I'm fine," she said, her voice pitched to an unbelievably cheery tone. "Didn't you promise me a date with Mr. Darcy?"

I'd wanted to tell her about my scent-stimulated hallucinations, and maybe now was the time. This was the first... er, vision I'd had about my best friend. Still...what if I was wrong? If I really did have a brain tumor, and these experiences were a symptom of being sick, then it would be stupid to worry Gilly. Besides, if she thought I was nuts, she might decide to tie me up, throw me in the car, and take me to the nearest emergency room.

But her avoidance of my question, in addition to the vision, stirred a bad feeling in the pit of my stomach.

"Tell me what's going on," I said softly.

Gilly took a sudden interest in a loose stitch at the bottom of her sweater, tugging on it to avoid my gaze. "We broke up." She paused. "Correction. I broke up with him." Gilly pushed up the cuff of her sleeve and revealed finger-sized bruises on her wrist.

"He did this?" I asked. My stomach clenched. What I'd glimpsed of Gilly and Lloyd's interaction had been real. Holy crap. Without thinking, I asked, "Was it something to do with Ari?"

Gilly gave me a sharp look. "How did you…" She shook her head then nodded. "I overheard him laughing with some of his buddies in the security office." Her hands were shaking now, and there was anger in her voice. "They were talking about Ari." Her eyes narrowed as her ire surfaced. "He called Ari a freak, and some other unsavory slurs that I won't repeat, because she happens to wear her hair short and the way she dresses."

I took her hand and gave it a pat. "He's an asshole."

"I marched right into that room gave him the it's-not-me-it's-definitely-you speech. He grabbed me and told me we were done when he said we were done."

"Is that after he told you he'd never let you go?"

Gilly paled. "Yes. How did you know that?"

Alarm kicked my adrenaline in. I skipped her question and went right to the important part. "That's a threat, Gilly. You need to call the police."

"And tell them what? Who's going to believe Silly Gilly over the head of security for the Rose Palace? Lloyd is an ex-cop, and he still has a lot of friends on the force."

"Yeah? Well, so do I."

"You mean your ex-husband chief of police who you haven't spoken to in ten years? That guy?" Gilly scoffed. "Shawn Rafferty didn't like me when you two were married."

Shawn and I had divorced for a myriad of reasons, but mostly because he'd changed his mind about wanting kids. I had not. When we divorced, we split everything down the middle, and since we didn't have children and we were both just starting our lives, I didn't sue for alimony. I didn't want anything tying us together anymore. Not even a last name, so I took back my maiden name. And then poof, like magic, it had been as if the five years we were married and the four years we dated never existed.

But say what you want about my ex-husband, he's a good cop. And, yeah, a good person. He and his wife had sent a lovely spray of lilies for my mom's funeral, and Shawn had even stopped in at the visitation. Our conversation, the first one we'd had since my dad had died a decade ago, had been short but not unpleasant.

"Shawn will believe you." I clasped both of her hands and looked her in the eye. "Promise me you'll call the police if that son-of-a-bitch comes within fifty feet of you again."

"We both work at the Rose Palace. Our paths are bound to cross." Gilly blew out a breath. "But I'll do my best to avoid him."

I stared at her hard, my mouth set in a grim line.

She raised her hand as if taking an oath. "And I'll call the police if he attempts to even talk to me." She pushed my shoulder lightly. "Now, come on. I didn't come over here to lament my tragic taste in men. You promised me a night of binge-watching Jane Austen movies, good wine, and all the popcorn I can eat."

My smile felt tight. Gilly was an adult, and she'd been living her life just fine for many years without me telling her what to do. "You're absolutely right. Let's fill up these wine glasses, and I'll start the popcorn. You break out the goodies." Like a weirdo, I loved mixing chocolate-covered raisins in with my salty popcorn. Yum.

Twenty minutes later, we were sitting on my comfy couch with throw blankets over our legs, a large popcorn bowl between us and honey buns on the coffee table. Our wine glasses were full of Cabernet Sauvignon, and our undivided attention was on Mr. Darcy.

"Why can't real men be like him?" Gilly bemoaned after Darcy gave Elizabeth moon eyes.

"No, thank you," I told her. "I like the fantasy of Darcy, but he's judgy and bossy and arrogant. Give me a guy who is genuinely interested in my happiness, and not what he *thinks* will make me happy. That's the guy I'll spend the rest of my life with." Not that I thought such a man existed. I wasn't content exactly, but I was resigned to living out my life as a single woman. I glanced at Gilly. At least, I knew I'd never be alone. Not with friends like her in my life. I nudged her and smiled. "Even so, I'll happily root for Elizabeth Bennet to get her man."

"So, you are looking for a man," Gilly said triumphantly.

"You're the worst," I said.

Gilly made a kissy face in my direction. "Best Bitches Forever."

High-beam headlights glared through my living room window. I shielded my eyes and waited for them to go off. They didn't.

"Who is that?" Gilly asked. "Were you expecting anyone?"

"No. Just you." I got up and looked outside with Gilly right behind me.

"Oh. Oh, no," she hissed. "It's Lloyd."

"Go lock the front door," I said. When she didn't move, I said with more force, "Now!"

Gilly took off toward the front door, and I moved quickly up the stairs to my bedroom, ignoring my creaky knees as I retrieved my gun case from my bedside table. My hands were trembling as I opened the case and grabbed my compact 9mm and a full clip of bullets. I loaded the gun while I returned to the front of the house.

It was dark outside. "Is he still out there?" I asked.

"Gilly!" I heard a man shout. "Gilly, come talk to me. I just want to talk. I'm sorry about earlier. I didn't mean it. I swear. I promise it won't happen again."

Gilly had her body pressed against the wall and out of sight. "I think he turned off the light so he could see inside," she said. "He won't stop calling for me."

"How did he know you were here?" An awful thought occurred to me. "The kids?"

"No," she said. "They're staying the night with friends." She shook her head. "I told him a couple of days ago that I was coming over here to celebrate your recovery." Her pitch went up a notch as tears flooded her eyes. "I'm so stupid."

"He's stupid. Not you."

"Gilly!" he bellowed. "Come out and talk to me. Don't make me come in there after you."

"That is just about enough." I loaded a round into the chamber of my pistol and stalked to the door. "Call the police," I said.

"I already did," she said. "What are you going to do?"

"I'm going to get that jerk off my property."

I unlocked and opened the front door, walking out with my weapon extended in front of me. The wind whipped my hair across my face, and I pushed it back with my free hand. I hadn't bothered to put on shoes, and the rough concrete from my walk bit into my socked feet. I ignored the discomfort as I took aim at the drunk in my driveway.

Lloyd, a tall man, handsome, even with a receding hairline, gave me a look of sheer incredulity. He wore a dark nylon jacket with a tear in the pocket, his cheek was red and swollen, and his lip was bleeding. I guessed this wasn't the first fight he'd started tonight.

"Get back in your car and leave, Lloyd. And stay away from Gilly," I said. "The police are on their way, and if you're gone before they get here, I won't file a complaint."

"You can't shoot me." He laughed. "Castle law means I have to be in the place you live. Otherwise, you'll go to jail for assault or attempted murder."

"The way I see it, I can shoot you, then Gilly and I can drag you into the house."

He walked up to me and pressed his chest against the barrel of my gun. "Go ahead, tough girl. Shoot me."

The sour scent of beer mixed with whiskey made my stomach roil.

I recognize his out-of-focus form before the reek of booze confirms it. "Bitch!" Lloyd yells. He grabs a red-haired woman, his hands encircling her throat. Like Lloyd, I can't make out her face, and with her knees buckled, I can't tell how tall or short she might be, but I can feel her desperation. She struggles to escape but he is too strong.

"Please," she whispers, barely audible. "You're...choking...me."

He throws her to the ground and straddles her, his thick hands squeezing her throat. But who's his victim? I'm helpless. She's dying. He's killing her.

I snapped out of it, full of rage. I lifted the 9mm higher and aimed at Lloyd's head. Something in my eyes must have frightened him because he took several steps back.

Sirens sang out in the distance.

"Tick-tock," I said to Lloyd. "A smart man would already be in his car."

He scowled at me. "Crazy bitch." On that note, he jumped into his vehicle, started it up, and squealed his tires as he reversed out of the driveway.

Gilly came running outside clasping a butcher knife. "Oh my gosh, Nora. You're a freaking superhero."

"When the police arrive, I'm filing a report," I said, trying not to pass out.

She whipped the knife around in the air. "But you told Lloyd—"

"Gilly, stop waving that thing before you hurt yourself."

She blushed as she dropped her arm to her side. "I forgot I was holding it. What are we going to say to the police?"

"The truth. Lloyd Briscoll is a bad guy, Gilly. Like, really bad." I shivered as pieces of the vision played in my head.

"He needs to be reported. And you need to show them your bruises. I have a feeling this man isn't going to leave you alone without encouragement."

Want more Nora Black? Click here!

"Sense and Scent Ability by Renee George is a delightfully funny, smart, full of excitement, up-all-night fantastic read! I couldn't put it down. The latest installment in the Paranormal Women's Fiction movement, knocks it out of the park. Do yourself a favor and grab a copy today!"

— —Robyn Peterman NYT Bestselling Author

"I'm loving the Paranormal Women's Fiction genre! Renee George's humor shines when a woman of a certain age sniffs out the bad guy and saves her bestie. Funny, strong female friendships rule!"

— -- Michelle M. Pillow, NYT & USAT Bestselling Author

"I smell a winner with Renee George's new book, Sense & Scent Ability! The heroine proves that being over fifty doesn't have to stink, even if her psychic visions do."

— -- Mandy M. Roth, NY Times Bestselling Author

"Sense & Scent Ability is everything! Nora Black is sassy, smart, and her smell-o-vision is scent-sational. I can't wait for the next Nora book!

— —MICHELE FREEMAN, AUTHOR OF *HOMETOWN HOMICIDE, A SHERIFF BLUE HAYES MYSTERY*

ABOUT THE AUTHOR

I am a USA Today Bestselling author who writes paranormal mysteries and romances because I love all things whodunit, Otherworldly, and weird. Also, I wish my pittie, the adorable Kona Princess Warrior, and my beagle, Josie the Incontinent Princess, could talk. Or at least be more like Scooby-Doo and help me unmask villains at the haunted house up the street.

When I'm not writing about mystery-solving werecougars or the adventures of a hapless psychic living among shapeshifters, I am preyed upon by stray kittens who end up living in my house because I can't say no to those sweet, furry faces. (Someone stop telling them where I live!)

I live in Mid-Missouri with my family and I spend my non-writing time doing really cool stuff...like watching TV and cleaning up dog poop

Follow Renee!
Bookbub
Renee's Rebel Readers FB Group
Newsletter

Made in United States
Cleveland, OH
20 July 2025